THE BLUDGEONER

The Toff moved silently through the dark garden.
The nearer he drew, the bigger and more powerful
the masked man seemed to be. His shoulders were
enormous, and he was so still he might have been
taken for a statue.

There was a sudden click of a door being opened.
The man squared his shoulders and raised his right
arm. Now at last the Toff could see that he carried
something heavy; it looked like a bricklayer's hammer with its massive steel head.

The door opened. As Naomi Smith stepped from
the porch onto the path, the waiting man raised his
weapon and leapt forward.

The Toff called in a sharp voice: "Don't move!"
On the instant the assailant spun away from Naomi
—and the Toff saw the murderous hammer swinging
toward his own bare head . . .

JOHN CREASEY
THE TOFF AND THE FALLEN ANGELS

LANCER BOOKS NEW YORK

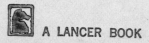

A LANCER BOOK

THE TOFF AND THE FALLEN ANGELS

LANCER BOOKS, INC. • 1560 BROADWAY
NEW YORK, N.Y. 10036

CONTENTS

CHAPTER 1

HOME TRUTHS FOR THE TOFF

It was a day when the Honourable Richard Rollison, known to so many as the Toff, was happy and content. Contemplating this state of near-euphoria as he sat in a comfortable armchair and looked idly at his Trophy Wall, he was puzzled. He had no right, he felt, to be as happy as he was; nor had he any special reason.

And yet he was in a mood when his heart was positively buoyant.

The world was in its constant state of fear and threat of bomb-blast, and the politicians who called themselves statesmen appeared no less impotent, and no nearer the use of reason.

The nation was in its constant state of tightening its belt and grinning, whatever new privation was thrust upon it.

The youth of the nation was under the usual, periodic charge of irresponsibility, the more mature critics virtuously recalling their own young days, which time and nostalgia appeared to have set in a permanent state of industry and innocence.

Taxation, especially for the Toff, who after some lean years was once again a man of major substance, was *very* heavy.

Yet he survived.

And the world survived.

And in Britain, most people lived reasonably well; the super-markets were full, the betting shops were busy and the football fans were about to put away their rattles, their team-colours, their scarves and their woollen hats, for this was the merry month of May.

Spring.

Suddenly Rollison laughed—a low-pitched chuckle of sound reflecting his good humour.

'And it isn't even love!' he murmured.

As he spoke, the door which led from the domestic quarters of his flat in London's Mayfair, opened, and Rollison's man-of-all-work appeared. His name was Jolly. He had served the Toff for so long that he had reached the stage of being more counsellor and friend than servant. There were some who regarded a gentleman's gentleman in this age of pop and do-it-yourself as an anachronism—as conceivably Jolly was. Indeed, he looked it, a man of medium height and doleful countenance, his sagging jowl hung in dignified abandon over a winged collar and a grey cravat. For the rest, he was dressed with impeccable restraint in a black jacket and striped trousers.

He carried coffee on a silver tray.

'Did you say something, sir?' he asked, putting the tray down on a low table near the chair.

'I said,' said Rollison, 'that I am happily out of love, and completely fancy free.'

'If I might say so, a pointer, sir,' remarked Jolly.

'Oh, is it?' Rollison looked surprised. 'And to what does it point?'

'It suggests the oncoming of—er—of—er——' Jolly, for once, was suddenly embarrassed and with remarkable presence of mind he moved back. 'I think I hear someone knocking, sir. Will you excuse me.' Swift and silent, he reached the door.

'Jolly,' called Rollison sternly.

'Sir?'

'There is no-one knocking. You were going to say that my mood of contentment suggested the final oncoming of maturity, were you not?'

Jolly looked at him judicially. 'Well, sir, it is to be expected.'

8

'Do I look my age?' demanded Rollison.

'But you are not *old*, sir!'

'That is a contradiction,' stated Rollison.

'In no way, sir. When I suggested that your—ah—maturer years made it possible for you to be content without any—ah —romantic interludes, I did not mean that you were—ah——'

'Incapable,' said Rollison drily. 'Or even impotent.'

'Indeed no, sir!'

'Jolly.'

'Sir.'

'Since you are in a mood to be devastatingly honest and I am in a mood to listen, tell me this: am *I* less attractive to women than I was? Or are women less attractive to me?'

Jolly hesitated, considered, then moved forward to pour out the coffee. As he handed a cup to Rollison he spoke again, as one stepping on very delicate ground. 'I think the truth is, sir, that you are more selective than in times past.'

'Ah. More choosey, you mean.'

'That is a more colloquial way of putting it, sir.'

'Yes, I suppose so. I had imagined that I had always been reasonably selective.'

'As indeed you have, sir,' said Jolly, earnestly. 'I am not expressing myself at all well this morning. What I mean is——' again he hesitated, and actually glanced upward as if hoping desperately for a celestial interruption. 'What I mean is——'

'What *do* you mean?' demanded Rollison, obviously not disposed to let his man off the hook. His expression was one of mild amusement, and his well-shaped lips were sardonically curved. He was handsome, with dark hair showing only a few flecks of grey; dark, well-marked eyebrows, dark eyelashes which threw the brilliance of his grey eyes into impressive relief. He was sitting back, relaxed, without a spare ounce of flesh, and obviously as fit as a fiddle. The tan of a brief holiday in the Swiss Alps still bronzed his face. He looked as if, when standing, he would be both tall and lean; as in fact, he was.

'What I mean, sir,' went on Jolly with great precision, 'is that you have always demanded beauty and a quick wit, but

9

recently you have not found these alone as satisfying as they once were.'

'Not bad,' agreed Rollison, smiling more approvingly. 'I'll settle for that.'

Jolly lost no time in withdrawing, and Rollison sipped the hot coffee, looking again at the Trophy Wall. He knew it was absurd and there was no reason for it, but he no longer felt that state of glowing contentment. His mood had changed to one of misgiving; the lightness of heart had been replaced by a sense of uneasiness, almost of burden. It was absurd! He finished his coffee and stood up, approaching the wall behind the large, pedestal-topped desk, and looked at trophy after trophy, almost as if he were seeking in each some memory which would bring back the mood he had just lost.

Or which Jolly had taken from him.

It couldn't be—surely it couldn't be—that he was conscious of his age? What man in his middle—well, just passed the middle-forties could feel that? He had never been fitter. 'Prime of life' was not an empty phrase but simply one of fact.

Could he do, today, what he had done in the days long past?

There was the top hat with a hole through it—he would have been dead had he not ducked in time. He could certainly duck as quickly today. There was an old hob-nail boot, one of his earliest trophies; to win that, he had fought off four men and hardly given the danger a thought—he would not relish the same odds today.

But he could face them, surely.

There was the curate's collar and the chicken feather, the phial of poison and the bicycle chain, the nylon stocking and the palm pistol, the dagger and the sword-stick. Each trophy —and there were fifty in all—was from a struggle against a criminal which he, the Toff, had won. All had brought danger, while in more than half the encounters he had been within an ace of death.

And in almost every case there had been a woman, young, middle-aged, or even old, who had attracted him and been attracted by him. To this day, he could not really understand why he had never married, why, for one reason or another, he had never—since the days of his incautious youth—proposed to a woman.

Yet he had known so many.

He believed—certainly he hoped—that all of them remembered their association with him with no regret at all.

He——

The telephone on the desk rang.

'And in time, too,' he said aloud. 'I'm becoming positively maudlin.' He lifted the receiver. 'This is Richard Rollison.'

'Good morning, Mr. Rollison,' said a woman with a most attractive voice. 'You won't know me. Though I have written to you. I would very much like to talk things over with you personally! May I?'

He said, without any noticeable hesitation. 'Is it an urgent matter?'

'I think it might be.'

'Then in half-an-hour's time?' suggested Rollison. 'Or else this afternoon.'

'I'm at the Mayfair Hotel,' the woman said. 'And in half-an-hour would suit me splendidly. Thank you.' And just when he thought she would ring off without introducing herself, she went on: 'My name is Smith. Naomi Smith.'

Smith, mused Rollison as he put down the receiver; Smith, Jones, Robinson or Brown, what did it matter? One assumed name was as effective as another. Naomi was not likely to be assumed, however. That had a ring of authenticity.

He moved towards the kitchen. The door which led to it was closed, suggesting that Jolly was preparing a lunch which would send an aroma into the flat if the door were open, so he closed it behind him, and tip-toed towards the kitchen, passing the main bathroom door on one side and the spare bedroom door on the other. Beyond these was his room; and further beyond was a passage leading to Jolly's room and the kitchen.

This door, too, was closed.

'Onions,' hazarded the Toff, as he turned the handle.

Lo! Onions were, indeed, frying, and giving off a splendid aroma. 'Splendid'—the woman on the telephone had said—

11

'Splendidly,' a rather unusual word in those particular circumstances. 'Very well' would have been more appropriate.

Jolly was at the wall-table, and there were traces of mince, potatoes, tomatoes and egg on a chopping board in front of him.

'Cottage pie,' announced Rollison.

Jolly started and turned his head.

'I—yes, that's right, sir.'

'Enough for three?' asked Rollison.

'Plenty, sir.'

'Be half-prepared,' advised Rollison. 'I had a telephone call from a woman stranger who will be here just after twelve, and if she measures up to those new standards you credit me with, she may be persuaded to stay to lunch.'

'Very good, sir,' Jolly said. 'I wonder——'

'Yes?'

'I've been thinking, sir.' Jolly went on, turning the shredded onions over with a wooden fork, 'that you have had a very pleasant spell of inactivity—comparative inactivity. You won't commit yourself to any course of action simply for the sake of having something to do, will you?'

'I hope not,' replied Rollison. 'Do you think I might?'

'I *have* known you feel that the moment has come to—ah —seek pastures new,' Jolly said. 'If you will forgive the expression. May I ask whether the caller said what she wished to see you about?'

'No,' said Rollison.

'In that case, sir,' said Jolly. 'I ask you most earnestly *not* to act precipitately.'

'I will ponder profoundly before taking any action whatever,' promised Rollison. 'I might even consult you.'

'Thank you, sir,' said Jolly, solemnly.

Rollison went out, closing the door meekly behind him. He went into his bedroom, off which a small bathroom led, and peered at himself in the mirror, then gave a broad grin, showing his very white teeth.

'That's right, preen yourself,' he jeered.

He went back to the Trophy Wall, but did not spend much more time at it. The past had lost its nostalgic appeal and he

12

was ready for tomorrow. Jolly was right in one way, at least —he hadn't been very active for a long time.

He wondered what Naomi Smith would be like. There was no reason, except the sound of her voice, why he should be looking forward to seeing her, but he was. He wrote three letters, to the secretaries of committees on which he served, including a London Branch of the Prisoners' Aid Society, and was sealing the last when the front door bell rang.

It was thirty-one minutes since Naomi Smith had telephoned.

He got up from the desk and waited for Jolly—it would be unkind to open the door himself, and rob Jolly of a chance of appraising the caller. From where he stood, the door leading to the domestic quarters was on the right, the door leading to a wide hall and the front door was on the left.

'Good afternoon,' said Jolly.

'Good afternoon.' The pleasing voice was unmistakable. 'Mr. Rollison is expecting me—I am Mrs. Smith.'

'Yes, Madam,' said Jolly, 'please come this way.' There was the closing of the door, footsteps muffled by the carpet, and then Jolly appeared and stood aside, announcing:

'Mrs. Smith, sir.'

Rollison moved towards the woman as she came in—and was almost shocked, for she was one of the plainest-looking women he had ever seen; her only redeeming feature, at first sight, were her fine, chestnut-brown eyes.

CHAPTER 2

FALLEN ANGELS

Naomi Smith smiled at Rollison, and something in her expression told him that she knew what had flashed into his mind, and was amused. She was dressed in a dark brown suit of good cut, with a most attractive figure. As she sat down he noticed her well-shaped legs, the skirt, which was short but not too short, the hand-made shoes, which were lighter than her suit but toned in with it.

As he took in these details, he moved towards a corner cabinet.

'What will you have to drink?'

'A gin and French, please.'

He poured out a whisky and soda for himself, carried the drinks across and sat down opposite her, the small table in between.

'Cheers.'

'Cheers.' Naomi Smith sipped. 'And thank you for your courtesy.'

Rollison gave a vague gesture of acknowledgement.

'How can I help you? . . .' As she stared at him with a curiously quizzical expression, he added, smiling: 'Or have you come to help *me*?'

She had a very good complexion for a woman in her forties, he reflected. He was beginning to like her. Almost at once he reminded himself that she might have come to beg or to borrow, even to con him. Back in his memory he remem-

14

bered a very plain woman named Belle, as convincing a confidence trickster as any he had ever met.

'No,' she said. 'I want your help.'

He should have been wary, but he was not.

'In what way?'

'It's a little difficult to explain simply,' she said. 'Will you bear with me if I seem to ramble?' she sipped again. 'I am the resident superintendent of a rather unusual hostel, for young women, and I am troubled by a situation which has developed quite recently. Something is frightening them, and two have left without any explanation. I could go to the police but if I did so there might be a scandal, and I'm sure that many of them would greatly resent it. And my control is positive but yet delicately balanced. I could undo in one day what I've done—or tried to do—over several years. These are not the easiest days for young people—or for those who try to help and guide them.' Naomi Smith paused, 'Have I made any sense to you?'

'In some ways, a great deal,' said Rollison. He considered, and then said tentatively: 'You run a hostel for fallen angels, I gather?'

Her smile disappeared, but not in disapproval.

'A very apt description.'

'Very special angels, I gather,' he said drily.

'They are indeed! And mine is a very special hostel.'

'Do you own it?' Rollison asked.

'No. I manage it for a group of people who are greatly concerned for these particular young women.'

'I see,' said Rollison. 'Is it a semi-luxury hostel?'

'In a way, yes.'

'Requiring certain qualifications,' remarked Rollison. He finished his drink, and gave a much warmer smile. 'Would it be better for you to tell me more about the hostel, rather than have me ask a lot of questions?'

She considered, and then answered:

'If you will answer me one question satisfactorily, I will gladly answer all of yours.'

'That's fair enough,' said Rollison, feeling more and more curious every moment. 'I'll try to be satisfactory!'

'Thank you. The question is, are you strongly prejudiced against young women whom you call 'fallen angels'? Do you condemn them out of hand as being beyond the pale?'

Rollison began to like this woman very much. He settled further back in his chair, placed the tips of his fingers together and appeared to look over the rim of nonexistent glasses. He contrived, in those moments, to appear a little like the caricature of a pedantic parson.

'No,' he said. 'I do not. On the other hand I don't see the wisdom or expediency of encouraging them unduly.' After a fractional pause, he went on: 'Is that satisfactory?'

'Yes,' she said, smiling again. 'Yes. Ask me whatever you wish.'

'Very well,' said Rollison. 'Will you stay for lunch?'

She was obviously taken aback, almost confused.

'How very nice of you! I——' there was another fractional pause. 'Yes, I would like that very much. Thank you.'

'I have a feeling we're going to need a little time,' said Rollison. 'Excuse me.' He pressed a bell-push in the wall by the fireplace where logs replaced the winter's fires. 'It won't be anything fancy . . . Oh, Jolly, Mrs. Smith will be staying to lunch.'

'Very good, sir,' Jolly said, and withdrew.

Naomi Smith looked at the doorway in which he had appeared for a moment, but repressed the impulse to comment on Jolly. She seemed to settle back in her chair, more at ease. Rollison, having had time to study her, found it difficult to explain his first reaction; she *was* plain, certainly, but somehow, when studied feature, by feature, there seemed no reason for the general effect.

She looked back at him.

'Exactly what would you like to know, Mr. Rollison?'

'I think I'd like to learn more about these angels. How many are there?'

'When we are full—twenty-five.'

'And they can all afford the hostel?'

'I don't quite understand you.'

'Isn't the kind of hostel you have described expensive?'

'The girls don't pay,' she said.

Rollison said, groping:

'You mean this is a state-sponsored institution?'

'No,' answered Naomi Smith, her expression changing as if something had touched her with disappointment. 'You *are* prejudiced against young people, aren't you?'

'Not knowingly,' replied Rollison. 'What makes you think so?'

'Your last remark made it sound as if you were about to say that it was time young people fended for themselves, instead of being spoon-fed by the state.'

Rollison chuckled.

'And that is exactly what I feel about some youngsters. Don't *you?*' The question came very quickly and there was a glint in his eyes.

She hesitated; and then laughed in turn.

'I suppose I do, about some. Have I given the impression that I—and the hostel supporters, are overindulgent towards the girls?'

'You have, rather,' said Rollison frankly. 'Will you have another gin and French?'

She looked speculatively at her glass, before saying:

'No thank you. Mr. Rollison——'

'Yes?'

'I really am deeply troubled, and I really think from what I've heard of you that you are perhaps the only man who both could and would help. It *is* true that the girls are indulged in some ways. The problem of each differs in kind, of course, and each one needs special treatment and consideration. I try to give both, but it is becoming increasingly difficult. I do *need* help.'

'What is so special about these girls?' Rollison asked gently.

'It is this: each of the girls has some very special talent, a talent which could be going to waste. Each—as you were so quick to realise—has had a most unsatisfying *affaire* with a man—or men. Several have in fact been married and deserted, most have had an illegitimate child. You might say as many do, that these young women have asked for trouble, that their rejection of the conventions has made them forfeit some of their rights in society. To me, that is not the most im-

17

portant factor. I do not simply say that these girls need the special care of society because in a way they have been victims of it. I believe absolutely that each should be, and can be, a wholly responsible person in her own right, and that most of these girls can be not only responsible for themselves but of value to the community. But that too is beside the point, as I see it.'

'Ah,' said Rollison. 'Is it very rewarding to help them?'

He saw on the instant that he had caused offence, but did not understand why: it had not been his intention. Naomi Smith's expression changed, she put her glass down, placed a hand on the arm of her chair and stood up quickly and with unusual grace. No-one had ever looked at him with greater intensity or directness.

'I really don't see any purpose in staying,' she said. 'Thank you for sparing some of your time, Mr. Rollison.'

She moved towards the door.

At the same moment, Jolly appeared in the other doorway, and said:

'Luncheon will be ready in five minutes, sir.' He realised what was happening and broke off, looking at the Toff as if pleading for guidance on what course to take.

Rollison waved him away and moved after Naomi Smith, who was half-way towards the front door. He passed her and put a hand on the door knob, but did not turn it.

'What did I say wrong?' he demanded.

'You know very well what you said.'

'I remember every word,' he admitted, 'but I can't see what made you take offence.' He turned the knob very slowly and with obvious reluctance. 'Certainly, none was intended, but if you feel as touchy over your young women as this perhaps it's better for me not to try to help. Presumably we would have to work together.'

He opened the door wide—on to a landing and a flight of stone steps; this old terrace house had been converted into four flats, one on each floor, of which this was the top. He was not angry, but troubled.

He had a strange feeling that this beautifully groomed, hitherto very composed woman was on the point of tears.

18

Certainly her eyes seemed to have become much brighter, and her lips appeared to be compressed to stop them quivering.

"Wasn't that remark intended to be taken literally?' she asked.

'I asked you if it were very rewarding to help——' He broke off as understanding dawned. His face relaxed and his eyes actually laughed at her. 'Now I see what a boner I dropped! It sounded as if I were asking if you were being well-paid.'

'It most certainly did!'

'It wasn't even remotely in my mind,' Rollison said earnestly. 'I really wanted to know whether you find it rewarding as a—as a vocation. I've somehow always associated guardians of fallen angels as somewhat more forbidding than you.' He put a hand lightly on her arm. 'Please come back.'

She averted her gaze.

'Thank you for explaining,' she said. 'I'm sorry I took offence.'

'It was an unbelievably clumsy remark,' said Rollison contritely. 'Would you like to tidy up before lunch?' He was leading the way back into the big room, only to lead the way out of it by the other door. 'Bathroom there,' he said, pushing a door open an inch or two.

She went in, her gaze still averted; and he felt sure that there were tears in her eyes.

He went back to the sitting room, puzzled and frowning. If she were really living on her nerves to the extent her reaction to the misunderstanding seemed to imply, how had she managed to keep up appearances when she had first arrived? He rang for Jolly. There was a spacious dining alcove one step up from the main room, and he drew curtains aside revealing a dining-table already set, Sheraton chairs and a long and graceful sideboard. Steaming vegetables stood on a hot-plate and there was a bottle of wine, the cork drawn. Before Naomi Smith returned, he had put two slices of Spanish honeydew melon on the table, laid so that two people could sit opposite each other.

He heard her coming. There were no signs of tears, now,

19

and he could have been mistaken before, although her make-up was suspiciously new. But her smile was bright. He handed her up the single step, drawing out her chair.

'Sugar or ginger?'

'I don't think I'll have either,' she said. 'It looks delicious.'

Rollison took a little ginger, and they ate, for a time, in silence. Then he asked with a gleam in his eyes:

'*Do* you find it rewarding?'

She drew a deep breath.

'It can be. But at the same time it can be—purgatory.' There was such feeling in her voice that he felt a kind of hurt for her. 'And when things go wrong, as they have done lately, I almost despair.' She hardly seemed to notice Jolly's soft-footed approach to change the plates, as she went on: 'They really are girls of exceptional talent. I am quite serious about that. The hostel was founded three years ago, when there was a scandal at a red-brick university. A dozen girls were sent down for drug taking, and a certain amount of sexual promiscuity. At the time I was the matron at one of the main residential houses, and four of the girls were under my care. I *knew* they were brilliant students. One was an outstanding architect, another had a positive genius for mathematics—oh, the details don't really matter. They all were sent down and disgraced, their studies cut off as with a knife. Several of the professors were greatly disturbed about the waste. They knew the decision of the President was both right and just, but they also knew the talents of these girls and were desperate to find a way of preventing them from being wasted.'

Naomi Smith broke off, as Jolly held the appetising cottage pie with its potato crust perfectly browned, in front of her. She helped herself but did not cease talking, so absorbed was she in what she was saying.

'One of the professors was—and still is—very wealthy. And the others were prepared to give private tutoring if the girls could be cared for nearby. All the girls were scholarship undergraduates, none had enough money without the government grant. And each leapt at the chance of going on with her studies. That's how it began.' Naomi went on. 'That was how the house of the fallen angels, as you call it, was

20

founded. In a way it's been a great social experiment and on the whole very successful. But I have a feeling—oh, I have more than a feeling, I *know* someone is trying to make it fail.'

She was now quite oblivious of Jolly and the dish of young carrots he was proffering, as she stared at Rollison as if challenging him to believe everything she told him: willing him to promise to help.

CHAPTER 3

A PROMISE FROM THE TOFF

Rollison flickered a glance at Jolly, who immediately began to serve their guest, while he looked very straightly into Naomi Smith's eyes, feeling great warmth for her.

'On the strength of your feeling,' he said, 'I will help if I can.'

Jolly's expression relaxed into obvious approval, and Naomi Smith caught her breath, as if the suddenness of Rollison's decision took her by surprise. But in a moment she was gripping his hand, and her eyes blazed with rare radiance.

'Oh, thank God!' she exclaimed. 'Thank God!' She held tightly for a few moments, then suddenly released him and turned away; for the second time her eyes were dimmed with tears. Almost blindly she picked up her knife and fork, beginning to eat as if she had no idea what was in front of her. 'I really didn't think you would, I couldn't believe you were all you're said to be.'

'I'm probably half as bad as my enemies say and half as good as my friends would like to believe,' Rollison said, to ease the tension. He paused, to eat; and Jolly came and poured out wine for the Toff to taste and approve. For the first time, Jolly was noticed; and smiled at. 'But the one person who probably sees me as I am is my Aunt Gloria,' went on Rollison.

'Oh?' said Naomi, blankly.

'She also has a heart of gold and a helping hand for fallen angels,' Rollison told her. 'So I've had some experience.'

'Good gracious!' exclaimed Naomi.

'Now what I need, and do take your time about it, is the full story of what is going wrong among your young women, and why you think that someone is trying to make the hostel fail. What do you call the hostel, by the way?'

'Smith Hall,' she answered.

Rollison's eyebrows shot up.

'Named after you?'

'Yes.' She was suddenly almost gay. 'It's a big old house in Bloomsbury, very handy for London University. The girls originally called it "Smith Hall" for a joke, now the name has become a fixture.' She went on talking, as she ate, with an easy control of words which Rollison found himself enjoying almost as much as he enjoyed the sound of her voice. 'The house was much too large for the half-dozen or so girls we had when we started and we used only the ground floor. Gradually we've opened all the rooms. It's been a remarkable success in a lot of ways—the sponsors put up the money for basic alterations and the fallen angels did all the decorating and arranging.' She paused. 'I *must* stop calling them fallen angels!'

'It sounds all right to me,' murmured Rollison.

Her plate was nearly empty and he got up and went to the hotplate.'

'Some pie?'

'I—oh, may I? It's very nice . . . They do their own cooking and the housework, too, it's quite remarkable how with a community of twenty-five there's someone good at every job . . . Even baby-sitting!' She looked up as if wondering how he would react to that.

'It seems a nice self-contained unit with the inevitable flaw,' Rollison remarked.

'Flaw?'

'Yes. No all-one-sex community can *really* be fully effective, can it!'

'No-one attempts to stop them from having boy-friends in,' said Naomi Smith. 'It really is a *very* modern establishment, Mr. Rollison.' She ate for a few moments and then went on: 'I suppose it isn't easy to explain attitudes. You see, my spon-

23

sors and I believe in the same fundamentals. The personal life of all individuals is their own, providing only they aren't a burden on, or a charge to, the community.' She looked at Rollison very straightly. 'Would *you* agree with that, Mr. Rollison?'

'I can see problems in living like it, but the theory attracts me,' answered Rollison. 'In this case, however, they *are* being a burden and a charge—if not on the community, then to a band of generous people. Naomi—answer me another question, please.'

'Of course,' she said.

'You aren't asking me to sponsor or go along with what you're doing, are you? You're simply saying that you need help because you're under some kind of threat which you can't handle yourself, and are nervous that if this threat gets out of hand it might lead to publicity of a kind you don't want.'

'That is the situation precisely,' she agreed.

'Good. What, also precisely, is the trouble?'

She finished eating and put her knife and fork down: he had already noticed how she gave herself time to think before answering any questions of importance; she was a most capable woman. Jolly appeared, as if by magic, cleared away and then produced a strawberry flan and cream as well as cheese and biscuits, and left coffee on the hot-plate. Rollison cut the flan into generous portions, as Naomi gave her answers.

'Two of the girls have really been frightened away.'

'*Frightened* away,' echoed Rollison. 'Help yourself to cream. Are you sure?'

'Yes. I'm positive.'

'Did they tell you so?'

'No, but they were obviously frightened, and until about two months ago, were thoroughly happy. They began to change. The whole atmosphere changed, there were quarrels and tensions which had never taken place before. I put it down to the infleunce of one or two of our new residents, but I couldn't really trace it to them. What was a happy community—and I mean that—has become tense and edgy. Good friends have become suspicious of each other. The trust that

24

once existed has almost completely gone. It—it's not really easy to explain in a short time, but I do assure you that it's happened.'

'You aren't doing so badly,' said Rollison drily. 'Have there been any thefts?'

'No, not so far as I know.'

'Then where does the lack of trust come in?'

'A creeping fear is a tenuous thing not easy to pin down. Each example of it, when reported, seems trivial. The young mothers appear now to be frightened of leaving their babies unwatched.'

'Do you mean the *babies* are hurt?'

'The mothers are afraid they might be.'

'But why?'

'That's exactly what I want you to find out,' said Naomi simply. She finished the strawberry flan on her plate, and looked at him again with that frank, penetrating expression he was becoming used to. 'In one way that's what most hurts and worries me. At one time they trusted me implicitly. They don't now. They don't come and confide or ask my help as they used to. They are as suspicious of me as they are of one another. I believe most of them would leave if they had anywhere to go, but they haven't.'

'Naomi,' said Rollison. 'Answer me another question. Do you really think that Smith Hall is in danger of being ruined —or are you afraid that you, personally, might be forced to leave and be replaced?'

She did not avert her gaze.

'I don't think it would be continued without me. I don't mean that I am indispensable in the actual work, but I don't think the sponsors would go on paying the cost if I were to leave. I can't be sure, of course, but Professor Nimmo assures me he would withdraw his support—and if he were to withdraw I'm sure the others would, too.'

'So you've discussed this with them?'

'Of course,' answered Naomi.

'Who are they, apart from Professor Nimmo?'

'There are four others,' she said, looking about her. 'Did you notice where I put my handbag? Ah, there——' she moved to get up, seeing the bag on the table by her chair in the big room, but Rollison, moving with almost startling speed, fetched it for her. 'Thank you.' She opened it, and took out a small, printed brochure. 'All the details are in there. We use that to show the girls whom we think could benefit.' She watched him glance down the list. 'Do you recognise any of them?'

He read:

Professor Arthur Nimmo	— Chair of Political Science.
Dr. William C. Carfax	— Chair of Philosophy.
Professor George Brown	— Chair of English Literature.
Professor Keith Webberson	— Chair of European Languages.
Dr. O. J. Offenberger	— Chair of Advanced Mathematics.

'I know Keith Webberson,' Rollison remarked, and reflected that he could get a completely objective report from a man with whom he had been both at school and at Oxford. 'And I've heard of Brown and Carfax by reputation—Offenberger is a new one on me. And these all give tuition free?'

'Yes.'

'Do any others?'

'There is a consultant staff of twenty-one.'

'Good lord!' exclaimed Rollison. 'You really go for it in a big way. And do all of these know all you've told me?'

'Oh, yes,' answered Naomi Smith. 'And much more—I've confided with them as the trouble has developed. And I know you know Keith Webberson—he suggested that I should get in touch with you. In fact he offered to approach you himself but I thought you might help for his sake and I wanted you to decide on—on the merits of the case as far as I could present them to you. And you really *will* help?' She seemed only half-convinced.

'I've no second thoughts,' Rollison said. 'I gather you've room for one or two more angels.'

They both smiled.

'Three, in fact—one of them left to get married last week, as well as the two I have mentioned.'

'If I happen to know of a young woman——'

'Oh, *no!*' cried Naomi Smith. 'You haven't——'

Rollison, pouring coffee, found himself spilling it as he spluttered with laughter.

'No, I haven't qualified a young woman to enter Smith Hall!' he said. 'But I have in mind one who is an angel aloft, as it were, and who is pretty bright at Social Science and has a good inquiring mind. By freak of chance, her name is Angela, and if I know Angela, she'll jump at the chance of joining you. As one of the girls themselves, she might win their confidence.'

'A new girl might, I suppose,' conceded Naomi. 'Of course —it's an excellent idea—my goodness! You believe in acting quickly.'

'But not fast enough,' said Rollison.

'I don't understand you.'

He covered her hand with his.

'The thought of waiting for another angel to come and settle in and then start investigating casts you down,' he said. 'You're so deeply worried about it that you can't wait to start. Isn't that how you feel?'

After another of her pauses, she said slowly: 'You really are a man of remarkable perception, Mr. Rollison.'

'Or Richard. Or Rolly—as you prefer. Angela apart, I won't be idle.'

'You mean you've other ideas already?'

'No ideas, but some experience,' answered Rollison. 'Have you a list of the names of the residents, their home and backgrounds and history?'

'Yes,' she said at once. 'It's wholly confidential, of course.' She opened her bag again. 'I can rely on you keeping it to yourself, can't I?'

'Yes,' said Rollison. 'Unless it reveals crimes which the police have to know about. If it does, I'll tell you first.'

This time, the envelope she handed to him was much bigger and bulkier. Inside were sheets of thin but glossy surfaced paper, and he drew them out. On the top left hand

27

corner of the first was a photograph of a girl with a wide smile—a brunette with shortish hair and particularly big and attractive eyes. The sheet itself was a copy made from an original typewritten document. There were entries under a variety of headings.

NAME:	Elspeth Jones
AGE:	22
SUBJECT:	Languages
NEXT OF KIN:	Father (Estranged)
NEXT OF KIN ADDRESS:	41 Senneker Street, Birmingham, 15.
OTHER RELATIONS:	See list attached.
MARRIED OR SINGLE:	Single—(1 child)—father unknown, Elspeth will not name him.
INCOME:	Nil.

There followed a brief case history of Elspeth Jones, who had been disowned by her widowed father when he had been told that she was pregnant. Rollison did not read it all, but skipped to the bottom paragraph, under the heading:

PERSONALITY AND TALENTS	A very pleasant and straightforward person with exceptional sense of loyalty. Without bitterness either towards lover or father. Lively, a good sense of fun, a good sense of colour and decor. Wholly trustworthy and likeable with a well developed sense of integrity.

Rollison looked up.

'Do you ever take in young women without being sure they are trustworthy and likeable?' he asked.

Without a moment's hesitation, Naomi said: 'Yes, of course. Smith Hall is not a place where people are prejudged. Some very unusual individuals are quite brilliant—all we do is create the conditions for them to study in their own specialised field. You would hardly complain if a man with a most unpleasant personality helped to find a cure for cancer would you? We have had some very off-putting girls, but as I said, until two months ago they all got along very well. Newcomers sometimes take some time to settle in, and are not always accepted quickly—that is one reason why I had momentary doubts about your Angela. Do you *really* think she will be prepared to help?'

'I'll know before the day's out,' said Rollison. 'And as soon as I know, I'll telephone you. That's a promise.'

CHAPTER 4

ANGELA

Angela's rosy cheeks were glowing, her blue eyes were bright, her plump and bouncy body seemed to quiver with excitement. She was short, only just five feet, but no one ever thought her small. Some called her a roly-poly and that, though old-fashioned, was very much on the ball. She wore a mini-skirt which rode high above her stalwart calves and trim ankles, and a loose-fitting scarlet jumper with a polo neck. Her hair, golden in colour, had a silken lustre.

'Gorgeous!' she gurgled. 'Absolutely gorgeous, Rolly. Bless you for thinking of me.'

'Knowing you, could I have thought of anyone else?' asked Rollison.

'I'd have hated you for life if you had. I've always wondered how it would feel to live branded by one's own indiscretions. The incredible thing is that it happens so much today. Anyone would think that reasonably educated angels would know this was the Pill Age.'

The Toff evaded that challenge neatly.

'So you'll do it,' he remarked.

'Rolly, darling, when can I start?'

'Very soon, I imagine. Tomorrow say?'

'Tomorrow is the day! Rolly, *bless* you! At long last I'm going to see how the other half lives.' She bounced out of her chair, opposite his in the Gresham Terrace flat, and kissed him on either cheek. 'Does Old Glory know about this?'

'Not yet,' said Rollison.

'I daresay that's wise.' Angela, suddenly even more ecstatic, sat on his knee and flung an arm round his neck. He needed no reminding that she was a very feminine young woman and fleetingly thought of his morning talk with Jolly. Angela simply regarded him as an uncle; masculine certainly, but hardly male in the exciting sense. She hugged him. 'You're the absolute pet,' she told him. 'Now I can have two of my life-long dreams fulfilled—to see the seamy side of life, and to play detective.'

'Angela,' said Rollison, regarding her severely, 'This is not a game.'

'Rolly, don't be silly, I know it's not.' She stiffened theatrically, holding him at arm's length. '*Richard*,' she said in the tone all the family used when about to disapprove of him. 'Don't tell me you think I'm incapable of being serious!'

'You're quite capable,' Rollison assured her. 'The point is, that this is one of those occasions to use that capability, and not indulge in the light-hearted frivolity you semi-intellectual young people find so necessary.'

'Of course, I gather that, and the fact that the wrong timing is the very snag over which your semi-intellectual angels have fallen.'

Rollison chuckled.

'Your point,' he conceded. 'Will you have another drink?'

'You mean, won't I get off your knee and allow you to breathe more freely.' She kissed him on the forehead. 'No, I won't have another drink and I won't play the fool any more. I'm absolutely thrilled at the chance, and truly grateful. And ——' she hesitated for a studied effect, then went on: 'I won't let you down.' She was suddenly all movement again, as she sprang off his knee like an india-rubber ball. She neither looked nor behaved like her twenty-four years. 'There's just one thing. What will happen when the others find that I'm not really qualified?'

Rollison looked at her solemnly,

'With a tum like that, no one would suspect you were cheating.' Before she recovered, he moved towards the telephone. It was five minutes to seven, and he was alone but for

Angela, this being Jolly's evening off. He dialled the number of Smith Hall, and Naomi Smith answered in that unmistakable voice which attracted Rollison in a way he had seldom been attracted before.

'This is Smith Hall.'

'This is Richard Rollison, to tell you that Angela is prepared to fall.'

'Oh, I'm *so* relieved,' said Naomi in a tone which was evident proof of her words. 'The more I think of it the more I like this idea. How soon can she come?'

'Tomorrow.'

There was a long pause, before Naomi said in a huskier voice:

'I don't really believe in you, Richard. You're like something spirited out of Aladdin's lamp.'

Angela, close to Rollison, was mouthing and touching her lips and her right ear, in imitation telephoning. Rollison held on for a moment, relishing what Naomi had said, and then asked:

'Would you like to speak to Angela now?'

'Is she with you . . . I'd love to.'

'Hold on,' Rollison said. He held the instrument out to Angela, then went out of the room. He did not want Angela to think he did not trust her to say what was wise, for beneath her high spirits he had sensed a moment almost of resentment when he had warned her that this was not a game. He could have listened-in on the kitchen extension or the one in his room or in Jolly's bedroom, but did not. Now that he was alone he was contrasting Naomi and Angela, and at the same time wondering what he had let himself in for. He could not even begin to think of a motive for what was going on. It could of course, he decided, be merely a matter of temperamental conflicts within the hostel. Each of the residents obviously had acute personal and probably emotional problems, and with high I.Q. was likely to suffer more from tension than folk who had a less highly tuned intelligence.

But Keith Webberson had sent Naomi to him, and Keith was no scaremonger, he must have some reason for anxiety. It was at least possible that Naomi Smith had not yet told him everything, wanting to make sure that he would help before unburdening herself of the whole truth.

He heard a faint click at the bedroom extension; Angela had rung off, he went to join her, and found her very much more sober, hardly smiling at all.

'Hallo,' he said. 'Problems?'

'No,' answered Angela. 'Not exactly problems, but Mrs. Smith made it clear that she is really worried. I'm going to see her right away, Rolly—she's waiting supper for me. Apparently that's how she interviews all her prospective angels.' A flash of humour brightened Angela's eyes. 'An angel who is about to fall salutes you!'

'I'll be around to pick you up,' promised Rollison.

Five minutes later, wearing a knitted cloak drawn tight around the neck, Angela was about to leave. As Rollison saw her to the door, he remembered how upset Naomi Smith had been that morning at that very spot. He held the door ajar.

'You're quite sure you want to go ahead?' he asked.

'Absolutely positive, no shadow of doubt about it,' answered Angela.

'You could run into a lot of troubles you don't expect,' he reminded her. 'Promise me one thing.'

'Yes, of course.'

'Tell me everything you find out, at least once a day, and if you've the slightest cause for alarm, let me know at once.'

'I will,' Angela assured him, earnestly. 'It's a chance in a million, and I'll make the most of it.'

He saw her down to the street door, and watched as she drove off in a shabby and battered Morris 1000, scarred from ten years of heavy usage. Yet the engine purred. She waved, tooted and was gone. He returned to the flat, in a curious state of uneasiness. Ought he to have encouraged Angela to go? Should he have made more inquiries first? What was the simple truth about his own view of the matter? That he was in fact inclined to think that this was not a criminal but an emotional affair?

He closed his front door, walked into the big room, and telephoned Keith Webberson, who had a flat in St. John's Wood. Webberson was a widower, a wealthy man whose life was dedicated to the spreading of knowledge and understanding throughout the world. He did this through his work, and he had devised methods of teaching English to illiterate people which were practised in much of the Commonwealth. And he did it also through voluntary organisations, serving on a dozen committees, including several attached to UNO.

The ringing sound went on and on. It was hardly surprising, Webberson was often out, but for a reason which he could not wholly understand, Rollison grew even more uneasy. He contemplated calling one of the other members of Naomi's group, but decided against it.

He tried to push the uneasiness away but it remained through supper, an indifferent Western and a bad documentary programme; even until Jolly came in, a little after eleven o'clock. He told Jolly what Angela had decided, was not wholly sure that Jolly approved. At twelve, he started to get ready for bed, and at twenty-minutes past the telephone rang. He lifted the receiver by his bedside.

'Rollison.'

'I've seen her, and I think she's absolutely remarkable,' said Angela. 'If it were only to help her, I'd go to Angel Hall.' She said that quite naturally, not as a joke. 'I'm moving in tomorrow. Aren't you pleased with your third-from-favourite niece?'

'I'm very proud of her,' replied Rollison.

'What a nice thing to say, even though its been wrung out of you. Bless you, Rolly!'

She rang off; and Rollison realised that she was now wholly committed. Slowly he finished getting ready for bed, but he did not get to sleep easily; he was more worried than he had been for a long time.

Angela telephoned about half-past six next evening; the Friday of that week.

'All's quite quiet, Rolly. I'm settling in.'

Keith Webberson did not answer the telephone that evening, either.

Angela telephoned on Saturday.

'It's a wonderful place, Rolly—perfect for what goes on here—but there *is* something wrong. I'll try to put my finger on it as soon as I can.'

'What kind of wrong?' he wanted to know.

'As soon as I know, I'll tell you,' said Angela.

Keith Webberson did not answer his telephone all that day.

He must be away, mused Rollison. 'And there's no reason on earth why he shouldn't be.'

But was that really true, in mid-term? he wondered.

Angela telephoned on Sunday and on Monday and Tuesday.

'I think I'm being accepted,' she said on Tuesday. 'There's one girl I particularly like—an Elspeth Jones, and I think she's bursting to talk to someone. I may have something more to report tomorrow.'

'How are you really finding things?' asked Rollison, before she could ring off. 'You've said very little, so far.'

'There isn't very much to say,' said Angela, obviously prepared. 'Nearly all of the others *are* suspicious of one another *and* of Naomi Smith. They seem to have a love-hate relationship. I can tell you one thing, Rolly.'

'What's that?'

'They may all be fallen angels but they all want to pick themselves up. At dinner time tonight they talked more freely than I've known them, it's almost as if they're beginning to forget that I'm new.'

'That's good,' said Rollison. 'Angela——'

'I really ought to go,' Angela interrupted. 'If anything happens worth reporting, I'll tell you afterwards. Bye for now!'

Rollison rang off, thinking almost ruefully that she had virtually dismissed him. Did that mean that someone had been —or might be—listening in? Or had she simply been afraid that someone would interrupt?

Angela telephoned again on Wednesday, and for the first time sounded almost excited.

'They are absolutely accepting me,' she cried. 'Two of

35

them confided in me last night about their own problems, and wanted to hear about mine. It seems to be far more difficult to invent a purple patch than a white one. I finally planked for a kind of grey. I can tell you another thing, Rolly.'

'What's that?' asked Rollison patiently.

'They're puzzled because they haven't seen Professor Webberson for a week—he usually takes one afternoon and one evening class at Smith Hall.'

'Isn't he away?' asked Rollison.

'He didn't say he was going away,' Angela informed him.

Rollison rang off, and immediately put in a call to Webberson; as usual there was no answer. On the spur of the moment, he went downstairs and walked to his garage, in a mews nearby, took out his latest car, a grey Allard, and drove to St. John's Wood. Webberson lived in a top floor flat of a block which towered above its neighbours; from south windows it was possible to see almost all of the ground at Lords.

Rollison got out of the lift opposite Number 901—Webberson's flat. Outside the front door was a printed note: 'No tradesmen until I'm back, please,' and it was followed by the initials 'K.W.' It was an odd way for an intelligent man to advertise the fact that the flat was empty, and Rollison studied the note, and then the front door—and on that instant decided to break in.

There was no convincing reason why he should suspect anything was wrong, but the suspicion was very strong in him. He drew on a pair of thin cotton gloves, not wanting to leave prints, then took out a knife with blades of highly flexible steel, and began to work on the lock.

CHAPTER 5

CRIME OF VIOLENCE

As he pushed the blade between the lock and the door frame, waiting for the moment when the tension on both sides, became the same and the lock would click back, Rollison felt a dozen questions tearing through his mind. Was this crazy? Was there really any reason to think anything was wrong? If a neighbour came out of one of the other three doors in sight, how could he explain what he was doing?

None of the questions made him hesitate.

As he worked, manipulating the blade with infinite patience, he listened intently. The silence was broken by a loud clang as the trelliswork inner gate of the lift closed. Almost at once there was a whirring sound, of the lift ascending. The odds against it coming to this floor were eight to one, but there was no way of being sure.

The lock clicked, and Webberson's door sprang open an inch.

The lift seemed to be coming very fast.

Rollison stepped inside the door and closed it, holding it tight with his left hand, for it would not close properly until the lock was repaired. Was this Webberson, by some strange freak of chance?

The lift stopped on the floor below.

Half jeering at himself but intensely relieved, Rollison put on a light, for the hall had no windows. A chair stood by a table against the wall and he placed the chair at the door; no one passing would now notice that it was open. There were four doors—one right, one left, two facing the front door. The parquet flooring was dull and looked dusty, as empty places will. A persian rug covered half the floor.

He opened the door on the left: it was the bathroom.

A towel lay in a crumpled heap on the floor, shaving gear was on a glass-topped table, and a safety razor and a shaving brush stood as if they had just been used. He looked at the brush, noticing the dried-up lather, matting the badger bristles—so it had not been washed after the shave. He opened the door opposite, into a kitchen, where a window overlooked an inner courtyard.

It was very modern and at first glance, clean. But there were cups and saucers and knives and forks, piled unwashed into the sink. A jar of ground coffee beans stood with the lid off, and a carton of cream, the lid partly on, was near it. Rollison poked at the lid, gingerly, using his finger nail. It was solid, with a minute line of mould growing at the edges where it had dried and drawn away from the side of the carton.

Rollison's breath was coming tensely.

He went to the right hand door facing the hall, which was ajar. He opened it wider with his elbow, and peered into a bedroom. This had the big windows overlooking lawns and parking places; a pair of trousers, carelessly folded, lay at the foot of the bed, a clean shirt was draped over a chair, clean socks were poked into shoes placed near. It was as if Webberson had put everything out so as to nip into the bedroom from the bathroom, and change. Some silver change and a wallet, keys, cigarettes and book-matches lay on a dressing-table which stood slant-wise, catching the light.

Rollison's heart began to thump, as he turned into the hall and the other room, the door of which was closed.

Webberson, lying in a crumpled heap by the telephone, was almost an anti-climax—not only after what Rollison had seen, but from the effluvium of decomposing flesh which met him as he opened the door.

Rollison stood in the bedroom for some time, recovering. He was accustomed to the sight of death, and normally unaffected, but this was the death of an old friend—and death by violence, for the back of Webberson's head had been smashed in.

Now, he had to decide what to do.

He saw the photograph of an attractive girl on a bookcase, signed: With love, Winifred. There was also a picture of an elderly couple, Keith's long-dead parents. There was nothing else of interest.

As he searched, he pondered deeply. He could call the police from here and wait for them—and admit that he had broken in; or he could leave, and call anonymously, and show a lively interest when the story broke in the papers. There wasn't much doubt of the better course, although he had to overcome strong prejudices. This was too much of a coincidence: it must be connected with the trouble at Smith Hall. If he were associated with it from the beginning, he would have staked a claim in the investigation. No one else need know, yet, what was happening at the Hall.

He decided to knock at a neighbour's, for the possibility of picking up a vital clue would offset the obvious disadvantage. As he stepped out of the flat he had a vivid mental picture of Angela's eager face.

What had he thrust her into?

Was she in danger even at this moment?

He rang a bell across the landing, and a middle-aged man answered, hovering near as Rollison used the telephone in the hall which was identical with Webberson's.

'Scotland Yard . . .' Rollison began. 'Mr. Grice, please . . . Yes, Superintendent Grice . . . What time did he go? . . . Will you call him at his home and tell him that Richard Rollison . . . R-O-L-L-I-S-O-N is at 901 Packham House, St. John's Wood and would very much like to see him here . . . Yes, I am an old friend . . . And will you also tell him that a murder squad is needed at the same address.'

'Hold on!' cried an operator, until that moment almost cynically uninterested. 'I'll put you through to Information.'

Rollison rang off, looking into the pale face of the neighbour, who was obviously badly shocked by what he had heard Rollison say.

It was hard to believe that Keith Webberson was actually dead; it almost numbed him.

'Did you say—say *murder?*' the neighbour asked.

'I did, I'm afraid,' confirmed Rollison.

'Who——' The man's voice was unsteady.

'Professor Webberson.'

'But—but he lives opposite!'

'He used to,' Rollison said quietly.

'Are you—sure?'

'Beyond all shadow of doubt,' said Rollison. 'Perhaps you will be able to help the police when——"

'Oh, *I* know nothing about it.' The man's voice shrilled.

'I'm sure you don't, but the police will want——'

'Toddy,' a woman said, opening the door of a room which was identical with the one where Keith Webberson lay dead, 'did I hear this gentleman say "police"?' She was middle-aged, fat as Angela would one day grow fat, blue-eyed, with pebble-lensed glasses. 'I—*oh*. Good gracious me. You're the *Toff*.' She drew a shuddering breath. 'Toddy, why on earth didn't you tell me? It's the Toff—Mr. Rollison. So—I *did* hear police. Oh, my goodness, what's happened. Is it the Professor? I said all along there was something funny about his going off without letting us know beforehand. I thought he'd gone off with that girl who's always there.' She peered up at Rollison as at an exhibit. 'Normally when he goes away he lets me know in time to arrange for the milk and bread and papers, it's most unusual—it's never happened before—for him to make his own arrangements. I was quite shocked when I saw the note pinned on the door. In fact I was quite put out—wasn't I, Toddy? I——'

There was the wail of a police siren, in the distance.

'Maud, the police will ask enough questions without you talking like this, do be quiet,' the husband rebuked. 'Surely they can't be here already, it's only been a few minutes since you telephoned.'

40

'The police don't take long, these days,' Rollison remarked. 'Thank you for letting me use your telephone.'

'That will be sixpence,' stated the pale-faced Toddy, primly.

Rollison looked blank, and then realised what was meant. 'Oh, for the telephone call.' He dug into his pocket for the coin, placed it on the table, and went out. The lift was whining, and he waited at the doorway of Webberson's flat until it arrived. Three men, two very large and one tall and thin, stepped out. Rollison recognised one of the large men as Chief Inspector Lumley, of the Yard's murder squad, a man with a big, bovine face and dark brown eyes. He looked a bully and a fool, but was, in fact, one of the kindest and most intelligent men of Rollison's acquaintance.

'Hallo, Mr. Rollison.' He spoke in a rough voice, with a twang of Cockney.

'How are you, Inspector?'

'I *was* having a quiet night! Where do you say we should go?'

'In here.' Rollison opened the front door, seeing the door opposite open a few inches. So Toddy, or his wife, was curious. Rollison led the way into the hall, and as the other followed, Lumley sniffed and the tall man said:

'Strewth! Not a new one, then?'

'Will you wait here for a few minutes?' Lumley asked Rollison. 'The rest of the team will be arriving soon.'

'Of course. I'll be here as long as you want me.'

There was a constant to-ing and fro-ing of men—photographers, a doctor, ambulance men, more detectives, some from the Yard and some from the Divisional Headquarters. After a short while there was a strong odour of an air-freshener, which somehow made Rollison more aware of nausea than he had been before. No one took any special notice of him although several recognised him and nodded or spoke. Outside the door was a uniformed policeman, and doubtless others were stationed down below. The police would soon hear if they hadn't learned already. Rollison, preoccupied with his own worry about Angela, did not find the time hang.

Perhaps an hour after he had first arrived, Lumley came out of the room where the dead man lay.

'Sorry to be so long,' he said. 'Mr. Grice will be here in a few minutes.'

Rollison said: 'The police never admit to being longer than that.'

'Well yes. But it's sometimes true. Will you tell me what you can—we'll go into the bedroom, they've finished in there. Soon have the body removed, too.' He led the way. 'I understand the dead man is Professor Webberson, of London University.'

'And an old friend of mine.'

'Sorry about that, sir.' Lumley's hard voice contrasted strangely with his almost soothing manner. "How did you get in?"

'I broke in,' answered Rollison simply.

Lumley looked startled. 'You broke——' he grinned, his face suddenly attractive. 'Just like you to admit it, sir! Why?'

'I couldn't understand why he didn't answer the telephone, why he wasn't taking his lectures and doing his usual work. On the other hand I didn't want to start a fuss if there was a simple explanation. So I forced the lock.'

'What time was this?'

'As nearly as I can tell you, nine-forty-five.'

'Were you alone?'

'Yes.'

'Where did you telephone from?'

'The flat opposite.'

'Then that'll be how the Press heard of it so quickly,' remarked Lumley. 'They're getting very impatient down below. Do you want them to know you found the body?'

Rollison smiled easily. 'You're being most considerate. I think on the whole, I do.'

'Then when Mr. Grice has been you can make your statement here and repeat it for the Press,' said Lumley. 'I——' there was a tap at the door. 'This is probably Mr. Grice.' Aloud, he called: 'Come in!' The door opened and another, younger man appeared.

'Mr. Grice is on his way up, sir.'

'Thank you,' said Lumley. 'Do sit down, Mr. Rollison.'

Rollison moved to the only armchair in the room, sat down and crossed his legs. The police were being almost too well-disposed; this might be because Lumley was naturally a pleasant man, or because he'd had instructions from Grice, or —and perhaps the most likely explanation—because Lumley wanted to lull him into a sense of security which Grice would shatter.

It was very unlikely that they would not at least consider the possibility that he knew much more than he had yet said.

The door opened, and Grice entered.

Now a senior Chief Superintendent at the Yard, Grice was a tall broad, spare-built man. His once brown hair, brushed flat and straight from his forehead, was greying, but his eyes were a clear hazel brown. The skin, stretched over his high-bridged nose, looked pale, almost translucent. On one side of his face was a scar from a booby-trap explosion which had been intended to blind the Toff. That had cemented a bond between them and they had ever since been good friends. But there were times when Grice, the police-man, came into direct conflict with Rollison, the 'amateur'.

Now, Rollison had a sense of impending conflict. It was in the brisk way in which Grice spoke, the quiet handshake, the intent scrutiny.

'Well, Rolly, what have you been up to?'

'Breaking and entering and finding the body of an old friend,' answered Rollison.

'What made you break in?'

'I was puzzled.'

'Rolly,' said Grice, very firmly, 'this is murder, it looks like a particularly violent murder, and there is no time at all for half-truths. Why did you break in? What made you suspicious?'

'Bill,' said Rollison. 'I had no reason at all to suspect that Keith Webberson was in danger. I was simply puzzled, and——'

'I don't believe you,' interrupted Grice. 'You didn't come here simply to find out if Webberson was all right. You had a stronger motive. What was it? What puzzled you?'

43

Here was the moment to tell the whole truth . . . and Rollison still had not made up his mind. But he knew that if he held anything back at this stage, then for the rest of the investigation he would be in conflict with the police, and it was the last thing he wanted.

'I can tell you why I was puzzled,' he said. 'The very simple truth. I'd been asked by a Mrs. Naomi Smith, who runs a hostel in Bloomsbury, if I would help her find out what was happening there. She told me that Webberson had suggested that she should get in touch with me. That was a week ago. For a week I've been trying in vain to get in touch with him. Then I learned that he hadn't turned up to give his usual lectures. As an old friend, perhaps his oldest friend, I felt justified in breaking in.'

He saw the quick exchange of glances between Grice and Lumley, as he talked, and felt an increasing disquiet eased only by the certainty that he had been right to tell his story.

'I'm very glad you broke in,' Grice said in a more relaxed voice. 'And I don't suppose we can blame you for not telling us about the hostel problem. Did you know that two of the residents were missing?'

Slowly, Rollison answered: 'Not missing. I knew they'd left.'

'They are missing,' Grice stated flatly. 'And we've reason to believe that one of them is dead.'

CHAPTER 6

MISSING—OR DEAD?

Rollison placed his hand on the arms of his chair and levered himself to his feet. He had another mental image of Angela, and he felt sick. Seeing his expression, Lumley and Grice exchanged glances again, and Grice spoke in an almost long-suffering way.

'What *have* you been up to? What haven't you told us, yet?'

'Didn't you once meet my niece—Angela Pax-Elliott?' asked Rollison.

'The pretty, roly-poly girl?'

'You've met her,' said Rollison.

'She plagued me for an hour, asking if there were any short cuts to becoming a woman member of the C.I.D.,' said Grice. 'What—my God! Is *she* a resident there?' Grice was filled with great alarm, and with surprise if not astonishment. After a brief pause, he went on: 'And if she was in trouble, why didn't she go to Lady Gloria at the Marigold Club?'

'In your cynical sense, she is not in trouble,' Rollison replied. 'She is satisfying her craving to play detective.'

'Well I'm damned!' exclaimed Lumley.

'Your idea?' Grice asked Rollison, grimly.

'Yes,' admitted Rollison. He moved to the window and looked down into the open space where the cars were parked —and he saw an ambulance move off. This was the one carrying the body, of course: what an end for a man like

45

Webberson. 'Yes.' He repeated, 'it was my idea, and at the time it seemed a good one. At least I arranged for Angela to telephone me once a day, and immediately if there is any sign of emergency.'

'Did you speak to her tonight?'

'Yes—and she told me Webberson hadn't been to his normal classes at the hostel, that really sparked me off. Bill—have you any reason to suspect other residents are in danger?'

'No,' said Grice. 'But I wouldn't like a daughter of any friend of mine to be there.'

'Have you any reason to believe that Naomi Smith knows that the girls are missing?'

'She reported them missing,' answered Grice. After a moment, watching the emotions chasing one another over Rollison's face, he went on: 'So she didn't tell you that.'

'She just said they'd left,' answered Rollison.

It wasn't really a lie, but how could Naomi Smith have any doubt that by keeping this grave aspect of the problem back, she had been deceiving him? He could see and hear her in his mind's eye: that beautiful voice and those lovely eyes and the earnestness of pleading. Why hadn't she told the whole truth? Hadn't she realised that if she had even hinted that the two girls were missing, he would have been more likely to agree to help? And why hadn't she told him when she had learned that Angela was going to take up residence—good God! How could any woman with decent instincts allow such a thing to happen?

'Getting angry?' inquired Grice, mildly.

'Simmering,' Rollison said. 'But as all good policemen say, first get all the facts. You won't raise any objection to my looking for the facts, will you?'

'No—if you undertake to pass on any you find,' said Grice.

'I'll pass them on,' promised Rollison grimly. He was seething rather than simmering, but at the back of his mind hovered the realisation that he was probably enraged as much because Naomi Smith had fooled him as because of the danger to Angela.

He wasn't really troubled for Angela: he could go and fetch her away now.

'One thing,' he went on.

'Yes?' asked Grice.

'What makes you think one of the missing girls is dead?' asked Rollison.

'A body was taken out of the Thames last night,' answered Grice. 'It had been there for ten or fourteen days and recognition under these circumstances isn't easy. But measurements match up with a Winifred de Vaux—D-E capital V-A-U-X,' he spelt almost mechanically. 'A dentist will check her teeth tomorrow morning, and we shall then know for certain.'

'And the cause of death?' asked Rollison.

'A savage blow on the back of the head,' answered Grice.

Rollison didn't need to say: like Webberson. He clenched his teeth, returned Grice's even gaze, and then asked:

'Do you need me any more just now?'

'No,' answered Grice. 'Unless you have the slightest idea why Webberson was killed, or know of anyone who might have owed him a grudge.'

'I haven't the faintest idea,' Rollison answered him.

'All right, Rolly,' said Grice. 'We'll keep in touch.'

His attitude, now, could not have been friendlier.

Rollison went out, aware that he was being watched by photographers and fingerprint men and the other detectives who were busy and intent. The lift was at this floor, a uniformed man opened it for him.

'Goodnight, sir.'

'Goodnight.'

It was quite dark, now—a quarter-past-eleven. How much could happen in an hour and a half. He remembered the Press would be outside but he hadn't prepared for the mass of them, twenty at least, crowded into the foyer of Packham House. The moment he appeared half-a-dozen flash-lights dazzled him, and others flashed as he closed his eyes to try to get rid of the dots of vivid white light in front of him.

'Did you find the body, Mr. Rollison?'

'Is this something new, or a development in a case you're already working on, Toff?'

'Do the police know who it was?'

47

'How was he killed?'

They flung question after question at him, and he answered most and parried some, unaffected by insistence. The sum total of what he told them was the sum total of what he had told Chief Inspector Lumley, and the police statement would certainly coincide. After five minutes and a breathless: 'Shan't keep you two minutes Mr. Rollison!' from a man who had just arrived with a television camera, Rollison pushed his way through the crowd, his expression unsmiling, though amiable enough.

He took his car out of its parking place, and switched on the lights, then turned into St. John's Wood Road, then into Finchley Road. A few people passed, walking. Two buses lumbered by, while private cars sped back and forth, their shiny roofs reflecting the light from the tall street lamps. He turned left, towards Swiss Cottage, and away from central London, and saw a motor-cyclist behind him, one who had been waiting near the block of flats. Thinking nothing of it, at first, he continued up the hill, towards the Pond.

The motor-cyclist still followed him.

He made a complete circuit of the block, and then headed back towards central London. In ten or at most twenty minutes he could be at Smith Hall. He drove slowly, and once past the brooding walls of Lord's cricket ground turned into a side street.

Rollison pulled into the side of the road, hesitated at the wheel, then put on the offside parking light, and got out. He was opposite a block of flats, and walked straight in. There was a hall, a staircase in the middle, a door marked EXIT on the right. He slipped behind this door but kept it ajar; and waited.

He heard footsteps, very light, almost stealthy.

A small figure appeared, topped by a white crash helmet, face half obliterated by goggles. Walking softly, this person crept to the stairs, looking to right and left. Rollison went out by the side door and strode quickly round to the front, re-entering the hall. The motor-cyclist was standing near the stairs, obviously at a loss. Rollison went straight up to him, shot out his hands and gripped him by the collar.

48

'Looking for me?' he demanded.

He was prepared for a kick, prepared for a twist or a wriggle, but not prepared for the startled gasp and the sudden, terrified stillness. And when he pulled the crash helmet off he was not prepared for the lovely cascade of fair and rippling hair.

'What—what are you doing?' the motor-cyclist gasped. 'Le —let me go!'

'Soon,' said Rollison. 'When you've taken off those goggles and let me have a good look at you.'

The girl put her hands up to her head and eased the goggles off slowly. The light was too dim for him to see the colour of her eyes but he could see she was young, perhaps no older than Angela. She was trembling a little but she did not try to dodge or run away, only stared at him in defiance.

'Why did you follow me?' he demanded.

'I—I didn't know you'd spotted me.'

'A blind man would have spotted you. Who are you?'

'I'm—I'm Gwendoline Fell,' she stated.

The name was vaguely familiar but did not immediately ring a bell. He let her go.

'You're lucky I didn't break your neck, Gwendoline Fell.'

As he repeated the name, he realised why it was familiar. She had a column in the *Daily Globe,* one of the most popular of the dailies, and also had a reputation for scathing comment and vitriolic personal attacks.

The realisation of her identity made him laugh.

'So you've realised who I am,' she said in a tart voice.

'Yes,' he said. 'I can't wait to read your column tomorrow. Is the *Globe* short of crime reporters, or did you just happen along?'

'I never "happen along",' stated Gwendoline Fell, drily.

'So you went with malice aforethought.'

'Certainly.'

'Will you tell me why?' asked Rollison.

At the back of his mind there was the thought that she might have been puzzled by Webberson's disappearance, even that she might have some knowledge of the trouble at Smith Hall. She was just the columnist to sniff out any kind of

49

scandal, and if there was one at Smith Hall she would make a righteous best of it, for she was a great champion of the young and the poor and the defenceless.

'Yes, I'll tell you why,' she said. 'I think you're a parasite.'

'You think I'm a what?' asked Rollison, and stared open-mouthed.

'You see, you can hardly believe your ears,' she said sardonically. 'You're so accustomed to your special kind of inherited divine right that when anyone tells you the truth about yourself, you don't even recognise it. You are a *parasite*, Mr. Rollison. You feed off the lives of others. You put on a cloak of altruism but in fact you're a——'

'Parasite,' interjected Rollison, recovering.

'That time I was going to say, an anachronism.'

'Oh. Out of date, you mean.'

'You know *exactly* what I mean. And when I heard you were at Packham House I couldn't get there soon enough. I've been *waiting* for a chance to put you under the searchlights. You have no right to usurp the duties of the police, for your own self-aggrandisement. Tell me—have you ever done a full day's work in your life?'

'Er——' began Rollison.

'Have you?'

'Er——'

'You know perfectly well that you haven't. You live off inherited money, you dabble in a few good deeds and make a few donations to good causes, you employ a fully able-bodied man who has pampered you all your life. You are a——'

'I cooked my own supper tonight,' stated Rollison, defensively.

'As I was about to say, you are an anachronism and a parasite in today's world.'

'Until you told me, I didn't realise it,' Rollison assured her. 'Tell me, do you always interview your victims this way? And do you always gather your evidence from hearsay and unreliable sources and then add a few fancy touches and consider the subject damned?'

'In the two years since I left university,' said Gwendoline Fell, with great deliberation, 'I have done more work and

50

helped society—people, *human beings*—more than you have done in your whole life. And you must be in the middle forties.'

'Do you know,' said Rollison. 'You've actually got one thing right. Don't forget to include that in your column, will you?'

'You no doubt think that's funny,' said Gwendoline, in an acid voice. 'I don't. Any man who seizes upon the murder of a friend to help him win more cheap popularity with people whom he has fooled for years is incapable of amusing me. I— *what are you doing?*'

'Proving how funny I can be,' said Rollison, controlling his sudden anger. He slid one arm at the back of Gwendoline's waist, and bent her double over his knee: and then six times in slow, deliberate succession, he spanked her with the flat of his hand—hard enough, he knew, to sting but not hard enough to hurt. She was taken so much by surprise that not until the fifth spank did she begin to wriggle, and at the sixth he picked her up and placed her on her feet again.

'Put that in your column, Gwendoline,' he said. 'And if you ever sneak up on me again, I'll repeat the dose.'

'My God!' she breathed in a voice choked with rage, 'I'll make you pay for this. I'll make you pay!'

She spun round and almost ran out of the foyer, and he stood staring after her, smiling, half-glad that he had acted so; but already half-sorry.

Then it came to his mind that for ten minutes or more she had made him forget all about Angela.

At least she hadn't been able to follow him to Smith Hall.

CHAPTER 7

SMITH HALL

Rollison drove more slowly than usual back to town, keeping a very sharp lookout, giving every car which appeared to stay behind him every chance to overtake. Satisfied that he had not been followed again he drove along Bloomdale Street, one of the few in the district where large single houses were still safe from the clangour of the demolition machines. Most of them were now used for business, university or hostel purposes; Rollison believed only one was still used as a private residence. There was some echo in his mind of a story about the owner, Sir Douglas Slaker—no, Slesser—no, but something like it. One of the old school, he had refused to sell any of the considerable properties he had in central London —oh, that was it! Sir Douglas Slatter, twice compelled by the law to give way to town planning schemes, more often successful in holding up what some called progress and he called vandalism.

Rollison had more than a sneaking admiration for him.

But he, Slatter, was an anachronism, too!

For the first time, he laughed at his treatment of Gwendoline Fell. Then he recalled that he had not remembered who she was, at first; his memory was failing.

'Don't be a damned fool,' he said *sotto voce*.

The big corner house, Number 31, was Smith Hall, the name and the number written on the fanlight over the front door, very clearly. There was no board in the grounds, nothing he could see to announce the fact that it was a hostel.

The house next door to it was Slatter's. He drove past, parking fifty or sixty yards away, then walked back to the hostel, glancing behind him all the time, still on edge because of Gwendoline. He had to step into the roadway at a spot cordoned off by flickering lamps outside a plot of land where builders were working but he hardly noticed it. He was about to turn into the gateway when he saw a shadow, thrown from a front room window light, on the ground. It looked like a man's head and shoulders. He walked on, without slackening his pace even for a moment. But he did not go far, just turned round and walked back towards Smith Hall very softly.

He could still see the shadow.

There was a low brick wall between the two gardens, and between the wall and each house perhaps ten feet. He turned softly into the garden of Number 29, thankful for the grass underfoot, which deadened the sound of his approach. He went along by the wall, and slowly the figure of a man materialised, waiting in the shadows and watching Smith Hall.

The nearer Rollison drew, the bigger and more powerful the man seemed to be.

Rollison, making no sound at all on the grass, drew level; only about four feet and the stone wall—no more than four feet high—were between him and the lurking man. Rollison watched and waited, just as the other was doing.

The man was obviously watching the front door of Smith Hall.

Anyone who came out of the Hall would not see him, and he would need to take only two or three quick steps forward to reach the flagged path. He was so still that if it were not for his breathing he might have been mistaken for a statue.

Had he a weapon in his right hand?

Rollison could not be sure, for the whole of the man's right side was in darkness, no light reached it at all. The left arm only could be seen, half-raised, the hand resting against the dark overcoat. And he was gloved.

His shoulders were enormous.

53

People passed, footsteps sharp on the pavement. Cars passed, mostly with only parking lights on, some with headlights dimmed, but bushes in the grounds of the Hall were so placed that the man was almost completely hidden; only the Toff, whose power of observation amounted to a sixth sense, would have noticed him.

There was a sudden click from the porch, as of a door being opened. The man seemed to square his shoulders, and to raise his right arm. Now at last Rollison could see that he carried something heavy, it looked like a bricklayer's hammer with its massive steel head.

The door opened; brighter light shone but did not fall upon the waiting man. Rollison placed a hand on the wall, ready to vault over, quite sure that he could forestall any attack. He saw the shadow of a woman thrown by the light in the hall, then heard the door slam and the light was dim again.

Naomi Smith stepped from the porch on to the path.

The waiting man raised the weapon in his hand, and leapt forward.

And as he leapt and as Naomi cried out in alarm, the Toff vaulted over the wall and called in a sharp voice of command:

'Keep still! Don't move!'

On the instant the assailant spun away from Naomi and towards the Toff, who now saw that there was a stocking drawn over the big face, making it quite unrecognisable. He saw, too, the murderous hammer swinging, not towards Naomi Smith but towards his own bare head.

Rollison flung up a hand to fend off the blow and swung to one side. He caught the other's forearm on his own, and it was like a steel bar. Off-balance, he tried to pivot, sensing that his assailant would rush at him, knowing that a man of such strength would be dangerous and could be deadly. He caught a glimpse of the stocking-covered face; it looked like the face of an idiot. Too near for a punch to be effective, Rollison gripped the other's wrist, and twisted in an attempt to heave the man over his shoulder. He failed. He caught a doubled knee, intended for the groin, on the inner side of his thigh.

He heard shouting: a woman, then a man, then several men.

He gripped again but the masked assailant pulled himself free, then swung away and leapt the wall, disappearing from sight, as two men rushed down the path towards Naomi Smith, who was standing like a figure carved from stone.

Voices broke, incoherently.

'What was it?'

'Where is he?'

'Is anyone hurt?'

There were a dozen useless questions while Rollison moved towards the wall and began to search the ground. There was so little light here. A policeman turned into the gate. As Rollinson bent down, a young man joined him.

'Looking for something?'

'Yes.'

'I've got a torch.' There was a click, and a pale beam of light wavered over grass and the dark brick wall—and then shone on the heavy-looking head of a bricklayer's hammer.

'What's that?' the youth darted forward.

'Don't touch it!' exclaimed Rollison, in time to make the other draw back.

Behind them, Naomi Smith was saying: 'I'm all right, I am, really.' On Rollison's right the policeman was bearing down and a number of other people had gathered in the gateway. Why did people have to stand and gape and watch when others suffered? What sadistic streak lay buried in man?

'Good evening,' said the policeman. He was slight but quite tall and had a faintly Scottish accent. 'What's happening here?'

'A man was waiting to attack whoever was coming out of the house, as far as I can tell,' answered Rollison. 'I happened to spot him. He dropped this.' He pointed to the hammer, glad to notice that the policeman bending down, made no attempt to touch it. 'The assailant got away.'

'Was anyone hurt?' asked the constable, practically.

'I don't think so,' said Rollison. 'Unless he himself was. This is a hostel for young women, and——'

'I know what it is, sir,' said the policeman, and lowered his voice. 'Aren't you Mr. Richard Rollison?'

'Yes,' said Rollison simply.

'Is this anything to do with what happened at St. John's Wood, sir?'

'From the look of that hammer it wouldn't surprise me,' said Rollison. 'Can you see that it's left there until your C.I.D. men come and have a look round?'

'I certainly can, sir.' The policeman pulled out a knob in the transistor radio tucked into his tunic and began to report to his division with a lucidity which Rollison admired, and which gave him much relief: he did not need to guide this young officer into doing what he wanted. And other police were approaching, from the gate one spoke with the patient firmness of authority.

'Move along, please, you're causing an obstruction. Move along.'

'Is anyone hurt?' floated from the gateway.

'Isn't that the hostel where——'

'Move along, now! I don't want to have to tell you again!'

'I'll be inside,' Rollison said to the constable near him, as the man pushed the aerial in.

'Thank you, sir. We'll have a car along in a very few minutes.'

Rollison looked towards Naomi Smith, who was now standing in the porch with the door behind her open and the light throwing her in dark relief. The policeman and the youth, seeing that they could do nothing more for her, turned towards Rollison.

'Are you *the* Rollison?' the youth breathed. 'The—the Toff?'

'Yes,' answered Rollison, crisply. 'Now I must look after Mrs. Smith. Why don't you telephone me later tonight or sometime tomorrow? You'll find my name in the book.'

'Oh—*may* I?' There was tremendous excitement in the young voice.

'I'd like you to,' said Rollison. 'And thank you for your

help.' He moved away, watched very intently now by everyone who was near, and joined Naomi Smith. 'Let's go in,' he said, and took her arm leading her towards the hall beyond.

No one was there.

Rollison noted that the hall was pleasantly bright and much better furnished than might have been expected. There were oil portraits on the wall; the chairs, an oak settle and a big wardrobe were all old and well-preserved. The parquet flooring was well-polished and there was a big Indian square—Mirzapore, Rollison thought. A central staircase ended at a half-landing from which another flight led to the right and to the left.

Looking down from a wooden rail were three girls. In the shadowy light up there, each looked pale and nervous and dark-eyed.

Why hadn't they come downstairs?

He wished Angela was one of them.

Naomi led the way to a room on the right, and switched on ceiling lights revealing a room which was part office, part sitting room. The big square desk had a green leather top, so did a smaller desk near it, on the right. On the other side was a typing table. Here were two telephones, a terra cotta jar filled with ball-point pens, another with finely-sharpened pencils.

Naomi, her hair ruffled, turned and faced him, her expression one of dismay and distress.

'I suppose you realise you might have been killed,' Rollison said in a conversational voice: there was no point in hectoring her, that would only worsen her distress.

'I—I do. I can't—thank you—enough.'

'You feared that two of your girls were dead, didn't you?' asked Rollison in the same, almost casual tone. 'Why didn't you tell me?' When she didn't answer, he went on: 'I could forgive a lot of things, but not that kind of deceit. You reported the girls were missing to the authorities, yet you came to me and asked for help because you said you didn't want to call the police.' As he spoke, he knew that what she had done made no sense. It wasn't simply that she had fooled

57

him—she had done something which was bound to come out, had lied knowing that the lie could not deceive him for long. What purpose could there be in such shortlived deception?

He was astonished at the change in her expression; agitation and a certain, unwilling deviousness could be read there.

She muttered, 'But I *did* tell you! I wrote to you!'

'You *wrote*?'

'Yes, last week—last Monday. I telephoned twice and there was no answer, and I was distrait. I—I gave it to one of the girls to post. I was terribly worried because Iris, Iris Jay hadn't arrived at the address she'd given me. Didn't you get the letter?'

'I did not,' stated Rollison flatly. 'Did you write it?'

He remembered suddenly a vague remark over the telephone about having written to him. He had hardly taken it seriously, accepting it as a social insincerity leading up to the request for an interview.

'Mr. Rollison,' said Naomi Smith, 'if you can't count on anything else, you can count on my absolute sincerity in wanting your help.' She was speaking hurriedly, as if to lead him away from the subject. Though he said nothing he was aware that she had not answered his question. Feeling came back to her voice and showed in her face again as she went on: 'But what does matter now, obviously you know. I—I'm dreadfully worried about Angela.'

Fear like a knife stabbed through Rollison's breast.

'Why should you be?' he demanded sharply.

'She—she went out, after dinner tonight,' Naomi told him. 'There was a telephone message from her to say that she'd discovered something I ought to know—would I meet her at the Oxford Street Corner House, main entrance. She would wait for me until twelve. That's where I was going, when——"

She caught her breath.

And Rollison stared at her, knowing exactly what was passing through her mind; the fear that Angela's call had served as decoy, and that going out in response to it had led her near to death.

58

CHAPTER 8

DECOY?

Rollison was acutely aware of three things. First, that although she was outwardly composed, Naomi Smith was in acute distress, and her mood was worsening. Second, that Angela was missing. *Angela,* whom he had sent here. And third, the chance that one of the residents had been trusted with a letter which she had not posted—unless, by some freak of mismanagement, it had been lost by the postal officials. He had to calm and reassure Naomi, and he had to find Angela *soon.* This was the only place to start.

He said: 'I could do with a brandy and soda. While you're getting it may I use your telephone?'

'Of course.'

She moved towards a cupboard near the desk, opened it, and revealed a row of bottles and several glasses.

Rollison dialled his flat, hard-faced. Jolly answered at once, and Rollison said: 'Miss Angela may be at the Oxford Street Corner House, Jolly—and could be in very great danger. Go and see what you can find out, will you? Tell the police if she doesn't turn up.'

'Of course, sir. At once.' Jolly certainly wouldn't lose a moment.

Rollison rang off.

There was brandy, which he really wanted for Naomi Smith much more than for himself. He joined her, seeing her hands trembling.

'Sit down,' he said, and poured brandy and gave it to her. He carefully poured himself a little, then drank with her. Before long the police would be here, and he wanted to hear what had happened before they arrived. The best way to learn would be by quick question and answer.

'Did Angela tell you she was going out?'

'No.'

'Who did?'

'One of the girls—Anne Miller.'

'Were they friends?'

'I—I think they get along all right. But since we've realised that Iris was missing, everyone—everyone's been nervous. I gave instructions that no-one was to go out alone, and that their boy-friends must collect them and bring them back. That's why Anne told me. Angela had gone off by herself—it wasn't simply breaking a rule to go out alone, it was walking into danger.'

It was so like Angela, too; she would be so sure that no rule applied to her, that she was free to come and go—it had probably not occurred to her that any risk might be involved.

'Did Anne have any idea where?' he asked.

'Angela—Angela hinted that it was to see a boy-friend.'

'Had she met any boy-friend before? Or gone out by herself before?'

'No. She was the last person I would have expected to——'

'I'm sure. You say she telephoned you?'

'She telephoned but I didn't speak to her. I was with one of the residents who's been very distressed lately. I was trying to soothe this girl, and Anne took the message.'

'Anne Miller?' asked Rollison sharply.

'Yes. Anne usually takes messages, she's really my secretary, I find her invaluable.'

'Was it Anne Miller who was supposed to post the letter to me?' asked Rollison, sharply.

'No, that was Judy Lyons. Judy *is* a bit scatterbrained, she could have—oh, I hardly know what to say or what I'm saying!' exclaimed Naomi, and she seemed almost in tears. 'Don't please start casting aspersions on the girls.'

'Naomi,' said Rollison quietly, 'you nearly had your head smashed in. Two of the girls are missing and might be dead. Angela, who is missing, was used as a decoy. A few aspersions here and there really don't matter. So you didn't speak to Angela yourself?'

'No—Anne did.'

'I'd like to see Anne, at once,' said Rollison.

'But—but——'

'Please send for Anne Miller,' Rollison grated; he had to fight against losing his temper.

Naomi hesitated, then put her brandy glass down with an unsteady hand and moved to the telephone. She picked up the nearest one, pressing a button beneath it; and almost at once Rollison heard a click, and the distant sound of a voice.

'Come into my study, Anne,' Naomi said. 'Hurry, please . . . I can tell you about that afterwards . . . Are they?' She seemed startled and now troubled by some additional worry. 'Very well, I'll go and see them when you're here.' She rang off, pressing one hand against her forehead.

It crossed Rollison's mind that this *could* be acting, but as she lifted her face and looked at him, he thought, no; she's in deep trouble and distress. His heart went out to her, but he did not show his sympathy, as he waited, hard-faced.

'The girls are terrified,' she said. 'I must go to the common room and talk to them.' She moved slowly away from the desk. 'They know about the attack outside, one of their boyfriends saw it, apparently—the boy with the torch.'

'Are there any other boy-friends here?'

'I don't know,' said Naomi. 'But Anne will.' As she finished there was a movement at the door. It opened to admit a tall, thin, sallow-faced girl with high cheekbones. Her dark hair, falling untidily to her shoulders, drooped over one eye. She wore a very short mini-skirt, emphasising slender but well-shaped legs. 'Anne,' went on Naomi Smith, 'Mr. Rollison wishes to ask you some questions. Give him all the information you can, please.'

Anne looked blankly—sullenly?—at Rollison, as Naomi went out, closing the door behind her. Anne did not move; the harder Rollison looked at her complexion the more like olive-coloured wax it seemed; and her eyes were the colour of dark olives, too.

'Did you speak to Angela Pax-Elliott tonight?' asked Rollison.

'Yes,' Anne said.

'On the telephone?'

'Yes.'

'What did she say?'

'She said she wanted to see Mrs. Smith.'

'Where?'

'At the Oxford Street Corner House.'

'When?'

'She would wait until twelve o'clock.'

'What else did she say?'

'She said she was on to something.'

'Were those her exact words?'

'They were her exact words,' asserted Anne Miller.

Not once as she had answered the swift succession of questions had her voice changed from a low, monotonous tone. And not once had she moved.

'What time did she call?' demanded Rollison, flatly.

'At eleven-seventeen.'

'How can you be so precise?'

'Because I am a precise person by nature, and I have a watch.'

'Did Angela sound alarmed?' asked Rollison.

'No.'

'How did she sound?'

'Excited,' announced Anne Miller.

'What was the name of her boy-friend?'

'Who said she *had* a boy-friend?' Now there was an inflection in the girl's voice which made her answer very nearly insolent.

'Didn't she tell you she was going to meet one?'

'She indicated it, yes.' For the first time Anne's expression changed and it was difficult to judge whether it was in a smile or a sneer. She had small but quite beautiful lips, spoiled with pale pink lipstick which jarred against the sallow tone of her skin. 'All of us indicate our romantic conquests whether they are true or not.'

'Lie about it, you mean?'

' "Hint" is a pleasanter word, don't you think?' suggested Anne.

'From what I know, delicate hints about boy-friends are hardly necessary here,' said Rollison, bluntly. He knew that his words were cruel but he had to break through this girl's resistance somehow, and it wasn't going to be easy.

She narrowed her eyes, but did not speak.

'Anne,' said Rollison. 'Do you know what's going on here?'

'No.'

'Did you tell Mrs. Smith that the other girls are terrified?'

'Yes.'

'Why are they terrified?'

'Do you think we should *welcome* having our heads smashed in?' demanded Anne, her voice rising to a cutting scorn. 'Or don't you think it matters, if such a thing happens to unmarried mothers?'

So he had hurt her, and had also loosened her tongue.

'I think it matters,' Rollison said. 'But weren't they terrified *before* the hammer attack on Mrs. Smith?'

'Quite possibly,' she said curtly.

'Then, *what was it that frightened them?*'

'Mr. Rollison,' said Anne Miller, as if suddenly overcome with weariness, 'I don't know what you're doing here or why you came, but I can tell you you're getting nowhere, fast.'

'*What terrified the girls?*' persisted Rollison, obstinately.

After a brief pause, Anne answered 'All right, then. There have been telephone calls from a man threatening to kill us. He always says the same thing—"just one blow will be enough, one blow on the back of your head." And then he rings off.' She half-closed her eyes but opened them wide again when he took a step towards her. 'Wouldn't *you* be scared?'

'Anyone would be,' Rollison answered gently. 'When did this all begin, Anne?'

'Three days ago.'

'And you've *each* had a call in those three days?'

'More or less. There's a telephone in each room, and we sleep three or four in a room. Whoever answered the telephone got the same message.'

'What has Mrs. Smith had to say?'

'She doesn't know about the calls,' said Anne.

'You haven't told the superintendent!' exclaimed Rollison, in astonishment mingled with disbelief.

'Can't you see she has enough on her mind already?' demanded Anne. 'We agreed we wouldn't tell her. She's warned us not to go out alone or come back alone. And she's called in the police. What more can she do? Of course we haven't told her,' she finished, in exasperation.

'If you had done so, do you think she would have gone out alone tonight?' asked Rollison, quietly.

'No one thought she was in danger,' Anne answered.

'How could you be sure *she* hadn't had a threat by telephone?' demanded Rollison, and when Anne didn't answer but looked appalled, he went on: 'Anne, who is doing this? Do you know?'

'My God, if only I did!' she cried. 'All I know is that we were happier than we'd been for ages. *All* of us. Can you imagine what it's like to be branded? Oh, we were fools, or else we deliberately defied convention, but we are branded. Even today you can stand at the window and see old women pointing and tut-tutting as they pass, and old men leering at us, and young men——' She was almost crying as she went on and the words were sharp and clear and yet every now and again her voice broke. 'Do you realise *why* we're here? We've got good minds, some of us are brilliant at our own subjects but we've offended the great god, convention . . . and we haven't even had the sense to look after ourselves. Our critics think we're immoral and our one-time friends think we're fools—*God*! And there isn't one of us who can turn to friends or relatives. Do you know what I was doing when I came here? I was a counter assistant at Woolworth's haberdashery department—and I was a child prodigy, they tell me there isn't anyone at my age to touch me in higher

64

mathematics. "That's one-and-eleven, please, penny change. Nail files? On the perfumery counter, madam. . . . That's seven-and-sixpence exactly, sir. . . ."'

'Stop it,' interrupted Rollison, sharply.

'I won't stop it! I *can't* stop it! I tell you I was nearly out of my mind when I heard from Naomi Smith. It didn't seem possible! A chance to study under Professor Offenberger and nothing to pay except time. There's even a creche here! We aren't under any pressure to have our babies adopted if we don't want to—God! It was like heaven! And then—and then the trouble began. First we had indecent telephone calls and beastly letters, then gradually the tone changed and we were told to go away from here. The very place we've come to love —oh, it's dreadful, it's dreadful!'

Rollison said briskly: 'Yes, Anne, it is. And it won't get any better if you keep a single thing back.'

He looked at his watch. It was half-past twelve and there was no word from Jolly and no interruption from the police. Jolly would have telephoned had he seen Angela, of course— so she hadn't gone to the Corner House. He had never really believed she had.

'I'm not keeping anything back,' Anne said, sullenly.

'Did you speak to Angela in person?'

'Yes.'

'Are you sure it was her voice?'

'Of course I'm sure, you don't think I could make a mistake about her, surely? She sounded excited, and very sure of herself. Has she been waiting all——'

'No,' Rollison said. 'I sent someone there as soon as I heard about the call. Anne, how well did you know Winifred de Vaux?'

It was a long time before Anne answered. She began to sway. Rollison took her arm and led her towards a chair, then poured out brandy. She lifted the glass, then lowered it again as she glanced up at him.

'Not—not really well,' she said. 'She wasn't easy to know. She—she was the only one here who really was obsessed with men, I don't think I've ever known anyone so over-sexed—so obviously over-sexed—and proud of it. Some would say she flaunted it, but she didn't, she was just proud. She thought it was glorious to be a woman. She—she's dead, isn't she?'

'It seems a possibility,' said Rollison. 'But what makes you think so?'

'The man who telephoned tonight said she was,' answered Anne Miller, her voice dead, stripped of emotion. 'And soon, soon, all the sluts and whores who lived here would be dead too.'

She tried to sip her brandy but her hand began to shake, and soon her slender body, until, inevitably, the tears began to fall.

And as she cried the door opened, and Naomi Smith came in.

CHAPTER 9

THE HAMMER

Naomi seemed to draw back when she heard the girl crying, then moved quickly towards her. She glanced at Rollison, and he expected to see scorn or reproach; instead she gave him a flashing smile, of thanks or congratulation. She put an arm round the girl and led her towards a chair. Rollison had not realised how tiny Anne was. He felt for the girl; he could understand her bitterness and her fear, but he feared for Angela with a kind of desperate self-blame.

As he stepped into the hall, Grice appeared from the front door, and they stopped, a few yards separating them.

'So you know nothing about this affair,' Grice said, accusingly. 'When are you going to stop trying to fool us?'

'The real question is the old question—when are you going to start believing the truth?' asked Rollison.

'Why did you come here?'

'You know why. And if I hadn't come, Naomi Smith . . .' he told Grice all there was to tell, and before he was through, knew that Grice had not seriously believed he had arrived with foreknowledge. 'Have you heard from Jolly?' he asked.

He hardly knew what answer to hope for.

'Yes,' said Grice.

'So—Angela wasn't at the Corner House,' Rollison said heavily.

'He gave her fifteen minutes, then called the Yard,' said

Grice. 'We had four men there within five minutes and a thorough search was made, but she wasn't in the place. Jolly went back to Gresham Terrace.'

'Have you put Angela on the missing list?' asked Rollison.

'Her description is with every division and every Home Counties force,' Grice replied. 'Her picture will be sent round tomorrow.' He paused, and then asked in a wary way: 'Do you want it to go to television and newspapers?'

'Of course. Why not?' asked Rollison.

'You must be very tired to ask that,' remarked Grice.

'Why should I—oh. The Press will know that she was a resident here, and do I want her picture to appear before the public gaze.' Rollison felt almost angry. 'Bill, can you seriously think I care a damn about gossip?'

'Your family might,' Grice said.

'Damn my family,' growled Rollison.

'Including Lady Gloria?'

'She is the one person who won't care a hoot.'

'Although if one of the family was in the—ah—was in trouble, surely the Marigold Club would be the first place for her to go,' said Grice. 'This could look as if Lady Gloria will extend the hand of charity to strangers but not to her own family.' Grice spoke with unusual feeling, and Rollison realised that he was trying to be helpful, trying to make sure that Rollison, so deeply involved, was seeing this situation objectively.

'Bill,' he said, 'arrange for the photograph in the newspapers and on televison, will you. And—thanks.'

'Right,' said Grice. 'I've a man waiting.' He strode to the front door and spoke clearly to a man whom Rollison could not see. 'Put all three pictures out to the Press and television, Soames.'

'Very good, sir.'

Grice turned back again, his manner easier, more matter-of-fact. He took a large wallet from his pocket, opened it, and took out a photograph which he handed to Rollison. Even though he first saw it upside down, Rollison recognised it at once: this was a photograph of a sledge hammer.

He turned it round.

'That was quick.'

'We can be quick,' observed Grice drily. 'It's probably the one with which Webberson was killed, too. There's a chip out at one corner, and it appears to coincide with an impression on Webberson's skull.' After a lengthy pause, Grice went on: 'Did you get any kind of mind picture of the man who was waiting here?'

'No,' answered Rollison slowly. 'Not of his face.' He considered, and then went on more briskly: 'Mind you, it was a very broad face. The features were squashed down by the stocking, but if I saw him again as he was then, I would probably recognise him.' He paused, then went on: 'He had little or no neck. I've never seen a man with broader shoulders and when he turned round on me I saw how deep-chested he was. A barrel-chested, bull-necked man at the peak of physical fitness, I would say.'

Grice was smiling.

'Not a bad mental picture,' he approved. 'I'll get that sent round at once—why didn't you get him? Distracted by Mrs. Smith's danger, were you?'

Rollison shook his head, very slowly.

'No,' he answered. 'He was too quick and too powerful, and I didn't give myself enough time.' He allowed a few moments for that to sink in, and then added: 'This man could crush one of the girls with his fist. Any sign of him?'

'None at all,' answered Grice.

'Footprints?'

'We've rigged up some floodlights but we're not getting much co-operation,' said Grice. 'We'll have to wait until morning before we've much chance of finding out which way this man went. At least he will have mud on his shoes, he was standing where a garden hose had been leaking most of the day.'

'I wondered what made the grass so wet. What's this about no co-operation?'

Grice, almost saturnine when he smiled in this dim light, said off-handedly:

'Sir Douglas Slatter does not approve of (*a*) the police and (*b*) the residents of Smith Hall. If he'd had his way our chaps would be driven off his grounds. As it is he won't allow us to use the mains electricity from his house for the flood-lighting—we had to send for more cable and run it off the supply here. Some of these old men are so prejudiced it's hard to believe.'

'Well, well, well,' said Rollison.

'What strikes you as so remarkable about that?' asked Grice.

'Sir Douglas doesn't approve of the place,' remarked Rollison, almost to himself. 'And he's not simply non-co-operative, he's actually obstructive. We're looking for a motive for the threats and the attacks, Bill. How is this for a motive: psychopathic disapproval of . . .'

Grice stopped him, abruptly.

'That's the wildest jump to a conclusion I've ever come across,' he rebuked. 'He's an old man, he's bad-tempered, he's not well and he was awakened out of a deep sleep. He'll be a different man in the morning.'

'Bill,' urged Rollison, 'have a look at the doorsteps leading into the back or side entrances of the house next door. If there are any footmarks, don't leave them to be brushed off in the morning.'

Grice contemplated him thoughtfully.

'That won't do any harm, anyway. I'll fix it.'

'Thanks,' said Rollison. 'Do you want me here for anything else?'

'No,' said Grice. 'Just one piece of advice, though, before you go.'

'I'm in the right mood to take advice,' said Rollison heavily.

'You've very strong personal reasons to stick your neck out,' said Grice. 'I've seen you before when you've a guilt-complex working like a computer in your mind. Don't stick your neck out too far, even for Angela. Think three times before you do anything off your own bat—and use us as much as you can. You may not believe it, but I'm as anxious to find Angela as you are.'

For the second time, Rollison warmed to the policeman.

'I believe you,' he said. 'And you'll watch this house closely, won't you?'

'A mouse won't be able to get in or out without being seen,' Grice boasted.

Rollison nodded, turned to the study door, which was closed, and tapped. There was a muted call of 'come in.' He found Naomi sitting behind the desk and Anne Miller lying back in a small armchair in front of her. She appeared to be all legs and long, loose hair, and had the face of tragedy.

'You needn't have any fear of being attacked,' he said. 'The police will make sure of that.'

'Yes, I suppose they will,' said Naomi, as Anne Miller looked up at Rollison from those sombre dark eyes. 'And there will be no way of keeping this out of the newspapers, will there?'

'Absolutely no way at all,' said Rollison.

Momentarily, Naomi Smith closed her eyes. Then she seemed to make a physical effort to pull herself together, braced her shoulders and spoke more crisply.

'Then we shall have to try to turn it to advantage. I've asked those of our sponsors who are free to be here at twelve noon in the morning, Mr. Rollison. I will be most grateful if you will join us.'

'I'll be glad to,' Rollison accepted. 'One question. How do you get on with your next door neighbour?'

'We don't get on,' answered Naomi Smith.

'*That* old lecher!' exclaimed Anne Miller with sudden venom. 'He used to think that all he had to do was open his window and beckon, and when he learned that we're in the baby business strictly for love, he started a virtue-and-hate campaign. Laughable, really. But—hateful.'

Rollison pulled up outside his house in Gresham Terrace, and decided to leave his car there. He did not feel like taking it to the garage and walking the five minutes back. A light was on in his living-room, and he saw the curtain move and a brighter light appear for a moment: Jolly had heard the car.

It was a little after two o'clock.

Jolly, dressed as if it were mid-day but looking very grey and tired, was at the flat door.

'This won't do,' said Rollison, with forced jocularity. 'We

71

can't have you losing your beauty sleep.' Then he saw Jolly's expression, a warning in itself, and realised that someone was in the flat. Inwardly, he groaned, for the last thing he wanted was another argument . . .

Unless this were news of Angela.

'Good evening, sir,' said Jolly. 'A Miss Gwendoline Fell called about an hour ago, and *insisted* on waiting.' There was a world of resentment in that insisted. 'I told her that there was no assurance that you would see her.'

'And *I* said you'd better,' declared Gwendoline Fell, from the inner door.

Rollison went in and looked across at her levelly. Her golden-brown hair was tumbled, her big blue eyes were tired, but she looked ready enough for battle. She also reminded him, rather strangely, of Angela.

'And what makes you think I wouldn't be happy to see her?' he asked lightly. 'Some coffee and sandwiches, Jolly.'

'At once, sir.' Jolly disappeared by the alternative route to the kitchen, and Rollison beamed down at Gwendoline.

'Come and sit down.' As they went into the big room, he added: 'Are you old enough to be offered a drink?'

'You really do have the most execrable sense of humour,' she remarked.

'Yes, I know. I'm sorry about that. What will you have?'

'What are you going to have?'

'I might have a spot of brandy in my first cup of coffee, to make it interesting and to wake me up.'

'May I have that, too?'

'Yes, of course.' Rollison looked at his large armchair longingly, and sat on a corner of his desk, with the Trophy Wall behind him. He did not need telling that the girl had come with serious purpose, and his respect for her had risen the moment he had seen her, for many a young columnist so disrespectfully treated would have assuaged her dignity by a vitriolic attack in print.

Perhaps she had done so.

'What brought you?' he asked.

'I heard about the trouble at Smith Hall and that you

saved Naomi Smith from having her head bashed in.' She spoke as casually as if she were recording the buying of a penny stamp. 'So I put in my stand-by column and postponed the one on you.'

'Pity,' he said. 'I was looking forward to reading about my parasitic and anachronistic way of life.'

'You might still do so.'

'You mean, if I do what you want me to do, you won't write scurrilously about me?'

'I never write scurrilously about anyone. And in any case, your background and your innate sense of superiority—of being untouched by such things as public comment—would protect you. No, I mean—I might change my mind about you.'

'Oh. Why?'

'You might get Smith Hall and Naomi Smith off the hook.'

'Oh,' said Rollison, and resisted a mischievous impulse to ask whether she was qualified to reside at Smith Hall. 'So you now know she came to see me?'

'And that you promised to help.'

'Who told you?'

'I've a friend who lives there—Judy Lyons.'

'Scatterbrain,' remarked Rollison.

'Who on earth told you she was a scatterbrain?' asked Gwendoline, in astonishment. Her expression changed and she went on: 'Oh, Naomi, I expect. Well, I talked to Judy on the telephone when the story came in about the trouble at Smith Hall, and she told me you'd made yourself quite a hero. And she said that Naomi seemed to think that you would and could help. So——' Gwendoline glanced up expressively. 'I thought you and I might bury the hatchet, and work together over this.' She glanced at Jolly who put a laden tray down on the low table at her side, and went on: 'The one certain thing is that you'll never solve this case on your own.'

After a moment of startled silence, Jolly drew back, looked at Gwendoline with a withering dislike, and said:

'I trust that will be all, sir.'

73

'Yes,' said Rollison. 'You go to bed.'

'Thank you, sir. If there is any word of Miss Angela you will wake me, won't you?'

'Yes,' promised Rollison.

'If you want to know where Angela is, don't go to bed yet,' advised Gwendoline. 'Because I'm pretty sure I know where she is.'

CHAPTER 10

TRUE OR FALSE?

Rollison moved from the desk, towards Gwendoline. Jolly, on his way back to the kitchen, stopped and turned round. The two men dwarfed the girl, and there was something almost threatening in their manner. Her eyes showed a sudden awareness of this.

'Where is she?' demanded Rollison.

'We have to make quite sure whether that statement was true or false, sir,' Jolly said, roughly for him. 'This young woman is quite capable of proffering false hope in order to get the information and assistance which she desires from us.'

'Yes. Where is Angela?' Rollison repeated, in a steely voice.

'I—I didn't say I was certain—I said I was pretty sure,' said Gwendoline, looking apprehensively from one man to the other.

'Where do you think she is?' demanded Rollison.

'Next door to Smith Hall, in Sir Douglas Slatter's house.'

'What!' gasped Rollison.

'I tell you that's where I *think* she is. Oh, for goodness' sake stop towering over me in that melodramatic manner!' exclaimed Gwendoline, straightening up abruptly. 'Angela suspected that some rather unpleasant telephone calls came from the house next door, and she found out that they wanted a housemaid. So she took the job. It's as simple as that.'

'Well I'm——' began Rollison, but his heart was lighter than it had been since he had first heard that Angela was

75

missing. It was so like her—to pretend there was nothing to report while she was working ingeniously and desperately hard to prove her capacity as a detective. 'When did you know about this?'

'Only tonight—from Judy Lyons. That's why I decided to come here, I thought you and I might come to an arrangement. If I put your mind at rest about your niece, will you give me inside information which no other newspaperman or woman can possibly get? I suppose it's too late to strike a bargain now,' she added resignedly. 'I—what on earth are you doing?'

Rollison turned away suddenly, and picked up the telephone and began to dial. He did not answer. His heart was thumping, and he was staring at the far end of the Trophy Wall, hardly aware of the old-fashioned cutlass or the bicycle chain in his direct line of vision; each had been used for murder.

'What *are*——' began Gwendoline.

'Please be quiet, Miss!' Jolly was sharp.

'This is Smith Hall,' a man answered Rollison.

'Is Mr. Grice still there?' asked Rollison urgently. 'This is Richard Rol——'

'Hold on, sir! He's just moving off!' There was a clatter of the telephone, and then silence, and at last Rollison turned to Gwendoline and Jolly.

'If she's at Slatter's place, I mean to find out. If the police won't search his house, I will.'

'Oh,' said Gwendoline, in a small voice. And then, while Rollison was still holding on to the telephone and Jolly, also tense, was watching him, she asked almost petulantly: 'May I have some coffee, please?'

Jolly opened his mouth as if in anger, closed it, relaxed, took a table napkin off a silver dish of sandwiches and poured out coffee.

'Hallo,' Grice said to Rollison. 'What is it now?'

'Bill,' said Rollison. 'I've just been told that Angela took a job as housemaid at Sir Douglas Slatter's house. If she did and she's there now, she might be in acute danger before the

76

night's out. Too many people now know who she is and what she's doing.'

'Yes, indeed,' said Grice, slowly. 'Hold on a moment.'

Rollison held on while Gwendoline, reaching for her coffee cup, stared at him; and Jolly, hot milk in hand, looked up from a half-stooping position over her.

'Yes,' repeated Grice. 'We'll have to find out. I wouldn't mind having a look round there, I've been thinking over what you said.' A chuckle fluttered his voice. 'I'll need a search-warrant, though and that——' Grice broke off, only to go on more decisively. 'I'll go and ask him to let me search and see what happens. If I have to get a search-warrant, what evidence do you have?'

'This time, will you just take my word for it?'

'I will, but a magistrate might not. All right, Rolly. I'll call you back in half-an-hour, don't come charging over here yet."

'If you're thirty-one minutes, I'll be on my way.' Rollison said.

Five minutes later, Sir Douglas Slatter, massive in a camel-hair dressing gown, and tight-lipped with bad temper, growled at Grice: 'If you have to I suppose you'll have to, but if you're doing it without a good reason I shall have questions asked in the House.'

'Thank you, sir,' said Grice.

He had four men with him and they went from room to room, with Slatter accompanying one couple and a middle-aged grey-haired housekeeper the other. Grice went out to his car, had a message telephoned to Rollison, and then rejoined his men. They had nearly finished, when he heard the housekeeper say to the two policemen with her:

'This is the last room—and there's a girl sleeping in it. A maid. Don't frighten her out of her wits.'

Grice reached them as she opened the door, and peered over their shoulders.

There, sleeping the sleep of the innocent, one bare arm over the bedspread, hair spread like leaves over the pillow, was Angela. She looked what she was: little more than a child. Grice eased himself inside the room and looked down at her closely. She was breathing evenly, her lips lightly closed. He gave a half-smile, of pleasure, and then withdrew.

Outside, he said: 'Now I would like to see the attic and the loft, please.'

Just after half-past three, Rollison's telephone rang again. It made Gwendoline start up from the chair in which she had been dozing, and as he lifted the receiver he heard the one on Jolly's extension lifted, too.

'Rollison.'

'She's all right, Rolly,' Grice assured him. 'She's sleeping naturally, and I didn't wake her. There's no-one who shouldn't be in the house, no sign of a man who fits the description you gave me, and no mud on any of the doorsteps. I'd leave Angela there. She's safe enough for tonight, anyhow, and I'll have that house watched as well as Smith Hall. We can decide what to do about her tomorrow.'

'Good enough,' agreed Rollison. 'The little devil!' But he laughed. 'Thanks very much, Bill, and goodnight.'

As he rang off, he heard Jolly's muted: 'Thank God for that,' and he saw Gwendoline by his side, bright with excitement, pretty as the proverbial picture. She clutched his arm and her grip was surprisingly strong.

'*Now* will you do a deal?'

'Yes,' answered Rollison. 'I'll do a deal and I'll see you get some inside information, but before we come to terms I'd like to sleep on the situation and see how I feel in the morning.'

'You mean, you're tired out,' said Gwendoline, giving way to a vast yawn. 'So am I! What time tomorrow?'

'Will two o'clock in the afternoon suit you?'

'Are you going to sleep *that* long?'

'I shall ask Jolly to see that I'm up by nine o'clock, I've a lot to do before going to Smith Hall at noon tomorrow,' said Rollison.

'Do you know,' said Gwendoline Fell, 'I think that given encouragement, you might be quite funny, after all.' She turned towards the door. 'Thanks for the coffee, and the sandwiches were lovely.'

Rollison went with her down the stairs; she was unbelievably light-footed and graceful; even when she threw a leg over her motor-scooter she showed grace. She placed her crash helmet firmly on her head and then shattered the street with the roar of the engine, raised a hand, and moved off at startling speed. Rollison watched her out of sight, then went up to his flat, and along to Jolly's room.

Jolly was in bed.

'Well, what do you make of that young lady?' asked Rollison. 'Do you trust her?'

'I grew to dislike her less as time went on,' admitted Jolly grudgingly. 'But I certainly wouldn't trust her too far.'

'No, nor would I,' agreed Rollison. 'Tomorrow, see what you can find out about her background and also about Smith Hall residents Anne Miller and Judy Lyons. Be discreet, and if necessary ask Mr. Grice for help. He'll probably give it gladly.'

'He is obviously deeply worried,' said Jolly. 'It's very hard to believe that Professor Webberson is dead, sir, isn't it?'

'Yes,' said Rollison heavily. 'Hard to realise that two of the girls are probably dead, too, and Naomi Smith is on the killer's list. At least he won't use the same hammer again,' he added. 'About nine on the morning. That will give us five hours' sleep, with luck.'

'I'll call you, sir.'

Rollison went to bed with so much on his mind that he half-expected to be a long time getting off, but in fact he was asleep as soon as he had adjusted the sheets and blankets. The reassurance about Angela, shadowed by the other murders, by the dangers, by the threats, had exhausted him.

Jolly brought him tea at five minutes past nine.

At ten o'clock he pulled up outside the modern severity of the new New Scotland Yard, was recognised and passed from constable to sergeant, sergeant to Chief Inspector and finally into Grice's office. Grice was not there. Three newspapers were open on his desk, an indication of sudden departure.

'He's with the Assistant Commissioner, sir,' said the Chief Inspector. 'He isn't likely to be long.'

'Thanks,' said Rollison—and the door opened and Grice

came in. He did not look in the best of moods, and simply nodded before rounding the desk and shuffling the newspapers into position. 'Good morning, Bill,' said Rollison. 'I wanted to come and say "thanks" in person.'

Grice grunted.

'The Assistant Commissioner doubts the need or the wisdom of my search of Slatter's house,' he said. 'Slatter's already been talking to M.P.s and they have been talking to the Home Secretary. Did you *have* to choose as suspect a millionaire who owns more property in London than any other single person?'

'No,' said Rollison. 'Angela chose him.'

'She has been seen in the house this morning,' Grice went on. 'I want you to find out why she went there as soon as you can, and if it's some damned flight of fancy, I want her out.'

'Yes, Superintendent,' said Rollison with tactful humility. 'Any news?'

'The sledge hammer was the one used to kill Keith Webberson.' Grice touched a file on his desk. 'It had been stolen from a building site nearby, a small block of flats is going up where there used to be a big house. No fingerprints, but there are burned initials on the shaft,' Grice added.

'What initials?'

'T.S.—and don't start jumping to any more conclusions.' Grice's interview with the Assistant Commissioner for Crime must have been very unpleasant. 'And don't ask me whether I'm trying to find the owner, either.' He moved his right hand as one of three telephones on his desk began to ring. 'Why should anyone try to murder Mrs. Smith, if we could answer that . . . Grice here.'

His expression changed as he listened, the sense of grievance died.

'Yes . . .' he said. 'Are you quite sure? . . . Well, now we know where we are. Is there any way of finding out whether she was killed by the same sledge hammer? . . . Yes, compare the wounds with those on the back of Professor Webberson's head . . . Yes, as far as I know I'll be here all the morning.'

He put the receiver down, and leaned back in his chair.

80

Rollison was almost sure what the main news was but he waited for Grice to deliberate, without trying to rush him.

'The body taken out of the Thames was Winifred de Vaux's,' he said flatly. 'The dentist has just given positive identification. There's no news of the other missing girl. Webberson was murdered about eight days ago—four or five days before the de Vaux girl disappeared. 'And——' Grice pulled at his lower lip before going on: 'And the neighbours across from Webberson's flat have identified the girl in the photograph as Winifred de Vaux. The woman recognised another visitor to Webberson's flat, too.'

Grice paused.

'The other missing girl,' said Rollison.

'The other missing girl, Iris Jay,' confirmed Grice. 'And Mrs. Smith was a regular visitor, too. So the two missing girls and the matron of Smith Hall were regular visitors to your friend's flat. Rolly,' went on Grice in a brisker, demanding tone, 'Was Keith Webberson one for the women?'

Slowly, Rollison answered: 'When he was younger, yes.'

'Do you have any reason to believe he grew out of it?'

'No,' admitted Rollison. 'None at all. But he was one of the group who sponsored this hostel. He——' he broke off, raising his hands, as Grice looked at him severely. 'Guilty conscience, do you mean?' he asked.

'It could be,' said Grice. 'It certainly could be. Mrs. Smith told me last night that you were going to be at Smith Hall when the surviving sponsors are to meet this morning. I don't want a man there but I do want a detailed report of what goes on.'

'I'll see you get it,' promised Rollison.

'Plain and unvarnished,' insisted Grice.

'Yes.'

'And by the way,' said Grice, 'I had a report that you had a late night visit from that columnist of the *Daily Globe*, Gwendoline Fell. What was that sly young woman after?'

'Sly?' echoed Rollison.

'Don't say she fooled you,' said Grice. He laughed with some show of irritation. 'But perhaps she did. She's twisted more of our men round her little finger than anyone I've ever known. Does she want inside information in return for her help?'

'William,' said Rollison with feeling, 'you get wiser and wiser and wilier and wilier every day. Yes, that is exactly what she wanted.'

'Be careful how much you tell her,' advised Grice. 'If I know her, she'll want a detailed report of the meeting of the sponsors, too.'

'Plain and unvarnished, no doubt,' rejoined Rollison. 'Bill, did you realise you had a lot in common with Gwendoline Fell?'

Grice looked astonished.

'I have?'

'Yes, you,' said Rollison. 'You share the illusion that I'm no longer capable of thinking for, acting for and looking after myself. I'll be in touch.'

He smiled broadly, and moved so swiftly that he was outside Grice's office before Grice had recovered from the impact of his words. And as he walked along the passages of the headquarters of the Metropolitan Police, he was humming to himself.

In less than an hour, he would be at the meeting of the sponsors; at least, of the four who were left.

CHAPTER 11

THE FOUR REMAINING

Police still watched outside Smith Hall, and were stationed at the corners of Bloomdale Street and Bloomdale Square, in positions from which they could watch Number 29—Sir Douglas Slatter's house—as well as Number 31. A few bystanders looked on with patient interest as Rollison approached; then a young newspaper photographer sparked their interest by crying out:

'Hold it, Mr. Rollison!'

There was a surge forward from the crowd, and an elderly man whom Rollison had known for years as one of Fleet Street's most astute crime reporters, came from behind the photographer.

'Good morning, Toff!' he said clearly, smiling.

Among the crowd the name was echoed: *Toff—Toff—Toff —Toff*, and on two or three lips it reached Rollison's ears.

'Good morning, Arthur,' said Rollison, above the noise of hammering from the nearby building site.

'What interested you in this—ah—establishment?' inquired the Fleet Street man.

'The murder of a close friend of mine,' said Rollison.

'Professor Webberson, do you mean?'

'Yes.'

'Did you know that he was a—ah—sponsor of Smith Hall?'

'Not until recently,' said Rollison. 'I did know that he was a man with an exceptional social conscience, and if he was a sponsor here, then Smith Hall was worth sponsoring.' He smiled again and moved on.

'If you'll spare just one moment——'

'I'm late already,' Rollison said, and turned into the gate. A policeman, young and obviously admiring, stood just outside. 'Good morning, officer. Am I the last?'

'One to come, sir, I believe.'

'Good. It's always nice not to be last!'

Rollison approached the house slowly, seeing it for the first time in full daylight. It was old, of weathered brick, ugly, but obviously spacious. It stood in its own grounds, like all the houses along here, but between the house itself and the walls dividing it from the other properties there was little more than a car's width. Beyond the driveway along which he walked were three green-painted garages. The brick wall he had vaulted the previous night looked newer than either of the houses, and the grass on this side of it was still damp. He glanced up at the first floor windows of the house next door— and a young woman slipped out of sight.

'All right, Angela,' Rollison said to himself, and he stepped on to the porch.

Another policeman stood just inside; Grice certainly wasn't taking the slightest chance. The door was closed, but opened before he had withdrawn his finger from the bell-push. Standing before him was Anne Miller; obviously she had been waiting for this moment. In broad daylight, she looked a little older. This morning, she had brushed her hair until it had quite a sheen, and her tunic-type suit was inches longer than the one she had worn last night. Her eyes looked huge, and there were dark patches under them—patches which should never darken the face of a young woman. The long, narrow face had a curious attractiveness; so did her small, exquisitely shaped mouth.

'Good morning, Anne.' said Rollison.

'Good morning, sir.' "Sir" was quite a concession. She closed the door, and went on in an almost conciliatory voice: 'I'm sorry I made a fool of myself last night.'

'Who told you that you made a fool of yourself?' asked Rollison.

'I didn't need telling,' she said drily.

'You need telling that when you open your heart and let the hurts pour out, you aren't making a fool of yourself,' Rollison told her. They stood together in that large hall with the portraits looking down on them, and he saw the shadows not only beneath, but in, her eyes. 'I was ready to help all I could before we talked,' Rollison went on. 'Afterwards I wasn't simply ready, I simply couldn't start soon enough!'

The way her face brightened showed both surprise and belief.

'You're—you're very kind.'

He squeezed her hand as the door of the study opened and a man said: 'We will have to start without them,' and Naomi Smith appeared, her eyes lighting up when she saw Rollison. But after a glance at him and a quick 'Good morning,' she said: 'Anne, if Dr. Brown arrives, show him straight in, will you?'

'Yes,' said Anne.

'Thank you, dear. Do come in, Mr. Rollison.' She opened the door wider and then stood aside, while two men standing by the fireplace, and one sitting on an upright chair with two hook-handled walking sticks, looked towards him. Nimmo, the physicist, tall, very thin, with a bald pate and a halo of grizzled hair, he recognised; Nimmo was standing by the side of a much shorter and much broader man, who had an iron-grey look about him—hair, eyes, suit, even his skin, appeared to be much the same colour. And there was something Teutonic about the shape of his head; Rollison placed him as Professor Offenberger, one of the few men whose renown as a mathematician was worldwide.

Naomi was introducing them, indicating each with a small wave of her hand.

'Mr. Rollison, I don't know whether you know Dr. Carfax.' Carfax, one of Britain's most renowned scholars, a leading pro-Shakespeare figure whenever Shakespeare's authorship was challenged, was sitting, so Rollison's identification of the others was quite right. 'Professor Nimmo, Professor Offenberger. I'm afraid Dr. Brown hasn't arrived, but as he doesn't answer his telephone he is presumably on his way here.'

'Unless,' said Offenberger, in a hard, near-guttural voice, 'he is also dead. Is that what you have come to tell us, Mr. Rollison?'

Carfax, who had a rose-pink complexion and looked a picture of health despite his infirmity, half-closed his eyes in patient resignation that anyone should say such a thing. Nimmo waved his hands in disclaimer.

'Nonsense, Otto, you have death on the brain.'

'That is the way it comes,' said Offenberger with grim humour. 'But I say we should already tell the police that George is late. How can we be sure all is well with him after these dreadful things? You know the latest, perhaps, Mr. Rollison? The poor girl, Winifred de Vaux, is dead—murdered like our good friend Webberson.'

'Yes,' Rollison answered. 'The police told me.'

'Did they tell you also who is doing these wicked things? Why every girl, and also all of us, are threatened with death? And it is no use raising your eyes to heaven, Will.' He turned his curiously iron grey eyes towards Carfax, who was certainly looking as if he were invoking aid from on high. 'We all of us are threatened. We take no notice, until the girls disappear and much worry there is. And now Keith is dead of the bloody——' he pronounced the word "bloddy"—'hammer, and Naomi's head is nearly smashed in. Do you deny it is serious? Do *you* deny it?' He pointed an accusing finger at Rollison. 'Do you deny we must stop the good works, that if we go on it will lead to more deaths? Tell me, at once, please. Do you deny the need for that?'

He still pointed and the others all stared at Rollison, as if he were an oracle.

"I—ah—am never happy about stopping good work,' Rollison murmured.

'But how can we the good works do if we are dead?'

'An excellent point,' said Rollison. 'Do you know who is trying to kill you? And do you know *why* anyone should try to kill you?'

'If we know, we tell the police,' rasped Offenberger.

Rollison's gaze moved slowly to the other men, and rested finally on Carfax, who looked almost cherubic, his fair hair concealing any streaks of grey, and whose head and shoulders and torso gave a remarkable impression of strength, in sharp contrast to the thin legs which dangled over the edge of the chair.

'Supposing you don't know, but only guess,' Rollison asked mildly. 'Would you tell the police whom you suspect?'

'It would be a waste of time,' said Carfax, his voice beautifully modulated. 'We believe——'

'You must speak for yourself,' Naomi broke in quietly.

'Yes, Naomi, I am doing so, and I speak also for Arthur, and probably for Otto. What kind of man would wage a war of persecution like this? Do we need to ask? We believe that the man involved is a fanatical bigot, probably extremely religious, who did his best to prevent us from launching this scheme, and when that failed has resorted to this hideous campaign. And the man we have in mind is so highly regarded at Westminster and in Whitehall, so immensely wealthy, that the police simply cannot agree as to his involvement. I speak, of course——' Carfax paused, to look round at each of the others, and received a nod from both men—'of Sir Douglas Slatter.'

'I simply cannot believe it,' Naomi said in a husky voice. She sat with both hands clasped tightly on the desk in front of her. 'I know he has been difficult, and that some of the girls imply he has made approaches to them, but they could have been—either wilfully or sincerely—mistaken. In their circumstances it is understandable that they should be suspicious and oversensitive.'

'If he's the puritanical fanatic Dr. Carfax suggests he might be, would he make passes like that?' Rollison wondered aloud.

'I've known some of these religious maniacs——' began Nimmo, only to break off. 'That isn't a fair thing to say. If a man's a pathological sex case, he can still be honestly religious. And we've something more than suspicion and prejudice to go on, Rollison. The lease of these premises is virtually up, and Sir Douglas, who is the landlord, will not extend it. I feel that the timing of these attacks is too much for coincidence.'

'I can see why you do,' agreed Rollison. 'Sir Douglas——'

'According to his own lights I believe Sir Douglas is a good man,' interrupted Naomi, stubbornly. 'Mr. Rollison——' She broke off.

'Will *you* check more closely on Slatter?' asked Carfax. 'You may not have the same prejudices as the police.'

'I shouldn't under-estimate the police,' Rollison said drily. 'So yes—I will see what I can find out about Slatter. But before I do—are you seriously considering closing down Smith Hall?'

'How *can* we go on?' demanded Offenberger. 'How is it possible? I have been warned like the others—stop coming here, finish the work—or you will be killed. I do not want to be killed. And I say to you all, let us not be obstinate. There are other girls, other men, who are very clever. These girls will be the loss, yes, but not irrepairable.'

'Irrepar——' Carfax began to correct, but stopped.

'Are they then?' Offenberger demanded fiercely. 'It has been a good and courageous experiment but this is not now a matter for private individuals. The brains of the country, they should be looked after by the country itself. Professor Nimmo has spent a fortune here, all of us give what we can but it is —no good. We stop. I vote for we stop.'

'Is that what you're here to decide?' asked Rollison.

'I'm afraid so,' said Nimmo, running a hand over his shiny pate, 'and although I don't like it, I think Otto is right. Unless we can put an end to this campaign of violence quickly, we must do what we're told.'

'I disagree,' said Carfax. 'And if George Brown were here, I think he would disagree. And I am not considering only the girls—I'm thinking that we owe at least something to Keith.'

After a short silence, Nimmo said: 'An unfair appeal, Will. Whatever we decide won't make any difference to the thoroughness with which the police search for the murderer. We won't be letting Keith down—or the dead girls, for that matter.'

'*Girls?*' exclaimed Naomi, shrilly.

'We don't really need telling that they're both dead,' argued Nimmo. 'Surely you aren't buoying yourself up with false hope. I——'

The shrill ringing of the telephone bell made them all start, and it seemed to ring on for a long time before Naomi picked up the receiver, it was almost as if she were afraid that this call would bring bad news.

'This is Mrs. Smith . . . Oh! Yes, he's here. Please hold on.' She looked at Rollison, and held the instrument out towards him. 'It's for you, Mr. Rollison—Superintendent Grice.'

'Ah,' said Rollison, taking the telephone. 'Thanks. Hallo, Bill.' This must be very urgent or Grice would not have interrupted the meeting, and his heart began to thump at the possibility that there was, after all, bad news of Angela.

'Can anyone else hear?' asked Grice.

'Not unless there is an extension,' Rollison said.

'No, that is the direct line,' said Naomi Smith hastily.

'No,' said Rollison.

'I thought I would give you this piece of news first, and you can break it to the others if you think the time is right.' Grice paused long enough for Rollison to wonder why he said "break it to"—and then he had a sudden flash of understanding only a split second before Grice went on. 'Dr. Brown was murdered last night. He was found slumped over the steering wheel of his car, in a deserted spot on Wimbledon Common. It looks as if he was forced to drive there by someone who had hidden in the back seat of his car, and struck from behind as he stopped.'

Rollison tried not to show the slightest reaction in his expression or in the tone of his voice.

'Do you know what time?' he asked.

'Yes—about ten o'clock, comfortably before the attack on Mrs. Smith,' answered Grice. 'Do the others there appear to be frightened?'

'Yes,' answered Rollison. 'Thanks, Bill. Will you leave this to me for a while?'

'Yes,' replied Grice. 'Not too long, mind.'

'Not too long,' promised Rollison, and rang off.

The others were concealing their interest in the call, and

he did not think they would have done so had they suspected what he had heard. He had no doubt at all what they would decide if he told them of Brown's murder, and it did not need Grice to emphasise that they could not be left in ignorance for long. There was only one way of preventing them from withdrawing their support, and that was by finding who was behind the murders. And if they were to keep Smith Hall and continue its activities, they would have to know quickly.

'You can't seriously suggest that Slatter is behind this,' Carfax protested. 'I can't believe——'

'Will you adjourn the meeting for, say, eight hours,' suggested Rollison. 'And I will pull out all the stops to investigate Sir Douglas Slatter's recent activities.'

There was only a perfunctory pause, before Nimmo gave the others the lead by a grave nod of agreement.

'Good,' said Rollison. 'Thank you gentlemen. But wherever you go, be sure you have a police escort. I have the very sombre duty of informing you that Dr. Brown was murdered last night, in the same way as Keith Webberson.'

After a stunned silence, Rollison expected Offenberger, at least, to make a passionate plea for retraction. But no word was said.

CHAPTER 12

ADAMANT OLD MAN

Rollison left the study, the expressions on the faces of the three men and the one woman vivid in his mind's eye; all were appalled. No one was in the hall, but as he glanced up at the gallery, Anne Miller appeared from one of the rooms, and raised a hand in greeting. He stopped and looked up at her.

'Any new problems?' he asked.

'It depends what you call problems,' she answered. She leaned over the wooden railing, her hair drooping downwards in a long, silken fringe, covering her eyes.

'Anything you find worrying is a problem,' he answered.

'Three of our little darlings have a rash this morning,' said Anne. "We think it may be chicken pox, and if it is they'll all get it. You haven't visited our Baby Farm, have you?'

'Not yet,' said Rollison.

'Then postpone your visit if you haven't had chicken pox,' advised Anne. 'Have you proved that our ancient neighbour next door is the murderer yet?'

'No,' answered Rollison. 'I'm just going to ask him.'

She gave a sardonic smile. The young policeman on the porch smiled too, as if he had heard the exchange. He watched with some surprise as Rollison walked to the wall and vaulted over it. The grass on the other side was much firmer, flanked by a drive and carriageway of grey macadam. The house appeared to be in immaculate condition. Rollison stepped on to the porch, which was supported by two white-painted pillars with the Number 29 painted on each, and rang the bell.

Light, quick footsteps approached—and Angela opened the door.

She gave a sharp, quickly suppressed, gasp.

'Good afternoon,' said Rollison. 'Is Sir Douglas Slatter in?' And as he spoke, he winked. The muscles of Angela's face worked as she tried to recover from the surprise.

'He, he's having lunch,—sir!'

'Take my card in, will you?' said Rollison, and he stepped past Angela into the hall. It was larger, yet not so impressive as next door, although at a glance the antique quality of every piece of furniture was obvious. 'Tell him the matter is urgent, please.'

Recovering her poise, Angela took the card, a little uncertain whether to show pleasure or fury at her uncle's unexpected appearance. Deciding to give nothing away, she turned towards a wide passage alongside the stairs, disappearing into a door on the right. There came a rumble of voices. Immediately, a massive young man appeared.

'Massive' was the word that first occurred to Rollison, as he noted the thick, bull neck, the powerful shoulders. Yet the man moved lightly on small feet.

'I'm afraid my uncle doesn't wish to see you, Mr. Rollison,' he said. 'He sees no purpose in a meeting.'

'Oh,' said Rollison, as if baffled. 'That's a pity. I thought it only fair to have a word with him before I went to the police.'

'You appear to spend most of your time with the police—judging from the morning papers. It really isn't any use, Mr. Rollison. He won't see you.'

Rollison frowned, looking even more baffled—and then, watching very warily, he moved forward, as if to pass Slatter's nephew. With a swift movement, showing reflexes at least as fast as the assailant's of the previous night, the young man flung out an arm, a barrier as firm as a piece of iron. Rollison, under no illusions as to the other's strength, grabbed his wrist, spun him round, and sent him crashing, halfway towards the front door. He did not look round but judged by the lightness of the thump that the other had fallen as an athlete should.

He went on, and entered the room from which the man had come.

Sir Douglas Slatter, sitting at the head of a table with his back to the long window, looked up with a laden fork only an inch from his mouth.

'Good morning,' said Rollison. 'I'm sorry if I chose a bad time.'

Slatter put his fork down slowly, and said, 'Get out of my house.'

'The moment I've said what I have to say——'

'Get out of my house, or——'

'No doubt you'll have me thrown out,' said Rollison pleasantly. He heard a sound behind him and moved swiftly to one side, so avoiding a swinging blow from the nephew. 'Do stop this young man,' pleaded Rollison. 'I really don't want to hurt him.'

'You don't want to——' Slatter caught his breath, and then said gustily: 'Guy—throw this man out.'

Rollison spun round on the instant, grabbed Guy's wrist, twisted his arm behind him in a hammer-lock so that he was utterly helpless, and smiled amiably.

'There really isn't any need for this horseplay,' he insisted, 'and I don't want to break this young man's arm—but I can do it as easily as you could smash his skull in with a sledge hammer.'

Guy had gone very pale. He was breathing hard, and as he faced his uncle, it was easy to realise that he was pleading with him.

Slowly, Slatter stood up.

Deliberately, he turned and went to a large fireplace and bent down, to pick up a brass poker. He held the poker by the handle with his left hand—and he raised it, more as a sword than a hammer.

'Let my nephew go,' he ordered.

'Or what will you do?' demanded Rollison.

'Break your neck.'

93

'With that? You might crack my skull, but——'

'I won't tell you again: let him go at once.'

He took a step forward. A larger man than his nephew, although he was nearing seventy he looked no more than sixty. There was no doubt at all that he was prepared to strike.

'You're a great believer in violence as a means to getting your own way,' remarked Rollison.

'You are a fine one to talk of violence. Let my nephew go.'

'I want ten minutes of your time. Give it to me, and I'll release him.'

Almost as soon as the words were out, Guy backheeled—an action for which Rollison was fully prepared. He dodged the kick with little difficulty, then pushed Guy's arm up a couple of inches further. Guy gasped, but managed to say:

'Don't—don't give in to him!'

'Blind courage and brute force,' said Rollison. 'They often go together.'

Slatter lowered the poker. His face was set in furious anger but his voice was even and controlled.

'I will hear what you have to say,' he said.

Rollison immediately released the young man, who moved slowly away, half-turning, so that he showed the pallor of his face and the sweat beading his forehead and his upper lip. He stood close by, holding his right arm.

Slatter put the poker back in the fireplace.

He looked at Rollison with nothing but acute dislike on his handsome face. 'Handsome?' Rollison asked himself. Certainly striking, certainly strong.

'What is it you wish to say to me?'

'It's very simple,' Rollison said. 'I want you to know that I have acquired a certain amount of evidence that suggests that you attacked Mrs. Smith last night—and that you killed Professor Webberson and Dr. Brown. Before I hand it over to the police, I want to hear what you have to say about it.'

'I have just one thing to say,' answered Slatter. 'It is ludicrous nonsense.' After a pause, he went on in a steely voice: 'And a second thing to say: I don't believe you have any evidence at all.'

'Don't you?' said Rollison.

'No, I do not.'

'*I* am the evidence,' stated Rollison.

'That remark makes no more sense than the rest of your assertions.'

'It will make sense to the police when I identify you as the man whom I saw attack Mrs. Smith last night.'

'Even the police wouldn't be deceived by such a lie,' said Slatter. He had a deep but not powerful voice and spoke with complete composure. If his expression said anything, it was that he had nothing but contempt for the man who had invaded his privacy and manhandled his nephew.

'If I make a statement on oath, not only the police but a judge and jury will take me seriously,' said Rollison. 'Even you cannot seriously doubt that.'

Slatter did not immediately deny it, and for the first time what might have been a look of apprehension showed in his eyes, but it soon vanished, and in an offhand voice which was slightly gruff, he said:

'You must make your own decision. You know well enough that it wasn't I.'

'I don't know anything of the kind,' said Rollison.

'Even *that* is a lie.'

'Uncle——' Guy began, but a glance from the older man silenced him.

'Is that all you have to say, Mr. Rollison?' Slatter had fully recovered his poise.

'No,' said Rollison.

'Will you please finish your charges and leave me to finish my lunch?'

'Will you grant an option to renew the lease of Number 31?' asked Rollison.

Slatter drew his heavily marked brows together in concentration, and then very slowly shook his head.

'No,' he said. 'I want them out.'

'To get them out you might have to get a court order and——'

'They wouldn't go that far,' interrupted Slatter. 'They are ready to pull out already.'

'Driven to it by murder,' observed Rollison.

'Driven to it by their own stupidity. However I will not bandy words with you. The answer is no, I will not grant an option, even if you offer to withdraw your identification of me as a criminal. That is a very cheap trick, Mr. Rollison—I nearly said that it was not worthy of you, but that would be paying you a compliment.'

'Why do you want them out?'

'That is my business.'

'Is inhumanity your business?'

'Mr. Rollison,' said Slatter, with great precision, 'I do not regard myself as a judge of what is humane and what is not. I want those harlots out of my house. They would never have gone there but for a trick—I was not informed of the kind of hostel it was to be. Hostel?' His voice rose. 'Or brothel? *You* no doubt know, Mr. Rollison.'

'Hostel,' said Rollison.

'I don't believe you, and nothing will change my mind.' Slatter held Rollison's gaze for a long time, and Rollison felt quite sure that he meant what he said. 'Make your absurd charges against me if it amuses you, but you are wasting your time, Mr. Rollison. I hope you realise that, and will now leave.'

'Do you really feel utterly indifferent about the infants next door?' demanded Rollison.

'No, I do not feel at all indifferent.' Suddenly, Slatter was enraged, even his cheeks were tinged with pink, and his hitherto cold eyes flashed. 'I am intensely concerned with them—determined that they will be taken away from the whores who brought them into this world and placed in the charge of proper authorities. Those women have no right at all to be in charge of children. They may care for them physically but their moral and spiritual life will be ruined. And——'

He broke off, drawing back a pace, as if some new thought had crossed his mind—and then he recovered, and to Rollison's surprise, put out an arm and touched him.

'I believe that to be true,' he said. 'I do not believe such women should have the custody of those children, but that is not the chief reason why I want to close the home down. Mr. Rollison, you are not the interfering braggart I believed you to be. I can see that you are motivated by genuine humanitarian reasons. Come with me—and I will give you a demonstration which will show you another side of this coin.'

'Uncle——' Guy began.

'You can come with me or stay and finish your lunch,' said Slatter. Now gripping Rollison's arm lightly he led the way out of the room and up the staircase. In spite of his surprise at Slatter's change of attitude, Rollison noticed the magnificence of a Rubens and a Gainsborough on the staircase, and at the landing saw a tapestry of deep colours depicting a medieval wedding—a piece probably unique. Slatter thrust open the door of a long, beautiful room, the walls of which were lined from floor to ceiling with books.

It was a scholar's room; a room for quiet thought and contemplation; a sanctuary.

Through the open window came the wailing as of at least half-a-dozen babies—and even from this end of the room it was easy to imagine that there were many more.

CHAPTER 13

MOMENT OF SYMPATHY

There were, in fact, only three.

Each child was in a separate pram, one high and old-fashioned, the others modern and low. Each was bellowing, his mouth wide open, plump dimpled cheeks crimson red. They were in a patch of the garden cordoned off with high wire, rather like a huge fruit cage.

No women were in sight.

The caterwauling seemed to grow in stridency and rage. The noise made a fourth, silent baby, also in a pram, seem oddly out of place. For he or she was sitting happily, or at least placidly, making no sound at all.

Rollison turned away from the wnidow.

'Yes,' he said. 'I see what you mean.'

'I have lived all my life in this house,' said Slatter. 'I was born here. I have worked and read in this room for over forty years. And for the last three it has been purgatory—absolute purgatory. If I were to extend the lease even by a week, by a day, it would encourage the young women to think that I might relent and allow them to stay permanently. I will not, Mr. Rollison. I have no peace at all. The only time when I dare have the window open is when I am not here to be disturbed. But even when the window is closed it is impossible to concentrate.' He placed broad, spatulate fingers on the window, and slammed it down. Only the placid baby looked up, with no great interest; the others went on crying and although the sound was less urgent it came clearly into the room.

'I trust,' Slatter said, 'you are now satisfied. Either they go —or I go.'

'Yes,' said Rollison again, 'there can't be any argument about that.'

'Do you seriously think that *I* should go?'

'No,' agreed Rollison, thoughtfully. 'Not on the face of it.'

'Nothing would make me leave this house. Nothing will make me allow those young women to stay there.'

'Young women—no longer whores?' murmured Rollison. Slatter made no comment.

'Sir Douglas,' Rollison said. 'I've heard it said that disappointment and frustration account for your attitude more than anything else.'

'Disappointment and frustration about what?' demanded Slatter.

'That you are not welcome to the beds of these young women.'

'Oh, nonsense!' Slatter waved an arm as if to wave the very suggestion away, but he seemed in no way annoyed. 'They will say anything to discredit me. I really do *not* need these promiscuous young women for any erotic amusement. I am surprised that a woman of integrity like Naomi Smith should allow her charges to make such wild accusations.' He moved towards the door, his back turned squarely towards the window. 'Now, do you understand my attitude?'

'I even have a very real measure of sympathy for it,' Rollison murmured.

'Any sane man would,' said Slatter. He turned slowly—as Rollison had noticed before, he had a slight stiffness in his left hip. 'Come and sit down.' He sat in a high-backed swivel chair and motioned Rollison towards another. 'As you are here, we may as well deal with this matter once and for all.' He folded his hands on the desk, rather as Naomi Smith had done. 'I know that I am said to oppose these young women on moral grounds. And indeed I do. But when I am not angry —and I was very angry when you forced your way in—I have to face the fact that this is part of a very much wider social problem. It is not simply a case of young girls being promiscuous—or unwise or unlucky—it is a case of the acceptance of free living by society. No particular girl is to blame. I am *not* pursuing a righteous vendetta against these particular young women. That would be intolerably unjust. I simply cannot continue to live here. In the beginning, I asked Mrs. Smith if she would move the creche—the cage was put there to keep out cats and other animals, but it wasn't practicable. There is no room at all, they would be right at the corner, with cars changing gear and passers-by always making a lot of noise.'

'So you were once on friendly terms with Naomi Smith,' murmured Rollison.

'Yes indeed. We were good neighbours. I sympathised in principle with what she was doing. I felt cheated, but not by her or by the young women. It was Professor Nimmo who negotiated the agreement. He knew perfectly well that I wouldn't have signed even a three year lease had I known what it was all about, so I blame him.'

'There *was* a great need,' said Rollison.

'Not next door to my house, Rollison!' Slatter's voice rose harshly but he recovered, unlinking his fingers, and putting his hands flat on the desk. They were big and powerful. His eyes had a penetrating directness as he went on: 'You see how angry I can get! However, there is now another side to this matter and a very grave one. *Is* it true that Professor Webberson and Dr. Brown have been murdered?'

'Yes. At least one of the girls, too.'

'It is shocking—quite shocking.' Something near to concern softened the stern features. 'And is it true that the man who was about to attack Naomi, before you intervened, was like me?'

'In the darkness, very much like you,' answered Rollison.

'Are you *quite* sure?'

'Like you and also like your nephew,' answered Rollison without hesitation. 'In fact, except for your features I could almost swear to it.'

'Except for——Good heavens, Rollison, if you can't

identify the features what possible means of identification is there?'

'Size—build—thickness of neck—height—speed of movement——'

'*I* can't move fast.'

'You can, to your right. What is the trouble in your left hip?'

'Osteo-arthritis,' Slatter answered impatiently. "Didn't you see this man's face? One of the newspapers says you could identify the attacker beyond all reasonable doubt.'

'Newspapers say a lot of things which aren't literally true,' replied Rollison. 'I could still go into the witness box and swear that the assailant was very like you and like your nephew.'

'I see,' said Slatter, his face set again. 'You are a long way from convinced, I can see. You think I could be a psychopath or even schizophrenic.' He pursed his lips and looked almost ugly, before he went on: 'What *would* satisfy you?'

'I think I could be sure if I saw you in a half-light with a stocking over your head,' said Rollison. 'And the same goes for your nephew. Has he lived with you long?'

'Certainly. He is my only relative,' explained Slatter. 'I have acquired great possessions and reasonable wealth and I do not wish to see them all swallowed up by that inanimate thing called the State. So this man used a nylon stocking as a disguise. If you can be sure——' He waved his hands. 'Oh, it is nonsense! How strong are the rumours that I am involved?'

'Quite strong.'

'Has any one of the young women made a personal charge against me?' asked Slatter.

'No.' Rollison did not think the time was right to tell what Anne Miller had said.

'And if indeed there was any truth in it, do you seriously believe that there would not have been complaints?' demanded Slatter.

'Yes, I do. The girls would keep quiet about it if they thought it could help them to stay next door.'

'Ah,' said Slatter. 'Yes, I suppose this is true. Well, there is

101

no justification at all for any charges, whatever you may say. Is there any other reason for you or the police to suspect me?'

'Not that I know of,' answered Rollison. 'Do you know of anyone who might want to make you look guilty?'

'I do not,' said Slatter forthrightly. 'I believe these charges against me are due entirely to the resentment the young women feel about my attitude—and I still believe my attitude to be completely justified. So!' He stood up very quickly, putting most of his weight on to his right leg. 'My answer remains——'

Across his words, very loud and clear, came a scream from outside; another scream followed. By that time Rollison was on his feet, leaping towards the window. As he flung it up he saw a girl in the doorway of the house, at the entrance to the cage, standing with her hands raised, staring into the cage. She screamed again:

'Anne! Anne!'

Rollison saw two things in the same moment. Anne Miller, appearing at the girl's side; and two small, dark creatures on one of the prams.

'My God!' exclaimed Rollison. '*Rats.*'

He saw Anne rush forward, shouting wildly and waving her hands; one of the rats turned and skimmed down the side of the pram, the other stared as if in defiance. Another girl appeared, then two or three more. One of them carried a tennis racquet, another a putting iron. By then Anne was within three feet of the rat still on the pram, and she continued to approach it although the stiffness of her movements showed how great was her fear.

The girl with the putting iron pushed past her and poked at the rat—and Rollison, one leg over the sill, wondered whether it would spring at her in a frenzy. Close to the window was a drainpipe, immediately below the jutting ledge of another window. He caught a glimpse of the rat scuttling away, before he turned his back on the scene, and climbed down; he supported himself against the window ledge, and then dropped to the ground.

A girl was crying.

A second had rushed to one of the babies and picked it up

with a gesture of desperation. Almost at once other girls went to the remaining babies.

Rollison reached the side door of the cage and opened it, but no-one seemed to notice him go in. Something started them all talking against one another, the only one who seemed to keep absolutely silent was Anne.

'I'm going *tonight!*' one girl gasped.

'We can't stay—we'll have to go somewhere,' muttered another.

'But we haven't anywhere else to go!' came from a realist.

Others were crying . . . more were talking, saying the same kind of thing.

'We've got to find somewhere.'

'It's impossible to stay *here.*'

'Did you see them? Actually on Donald's pram.'

'Two *huge* rats.'

'I once heard of a rat——'

'For heaven's sake be quiet, Chloe!'

'How—how did they get in?'

'Yes—how did they get in?' demanded another. 'There must be a hole in the netting.'

Immediately, several of the girls began to scan the foot of the cage, which Rollison was already doing. So far he had found no break—no sign of anything which was large enough for a mouse to have got through. Several of the girls saw and recognised him, one or two said 'hallo.' Slatter was still watching from his study window. A policeman appeared at the door leading from the house, followed by a second, who made a bee-line for Rollison.

'Did you see what happened, sir?'

'I saw two rats but I didn't see how they got in,' answered Rollison. 'And the wire doesn't seem to be broken.'

'Been a lot of rats since they pulled down that old house and started building,' the policeman said.

Then Rollison saw a hole almost at shoulder height and not two feet away from the policeman's face. The man turned. The girls were still talking, some were trying to soothe and reassure the others. The girl who had first raised the alarm was now by Anne, who held one of the children in her arms.

'My God!' breathed the policeman. 'Look at that.'

He was looking at the spot which had caught Rollison's attention—a round hole cut in the strands of the wire. It had obviously been done recently, there were shiny surfaces to some of the cut strands, catching the sun. It was about the size of a football, perhaps a little smaller, and a dozen rats could have got through there.

'They were placed inside all right,' the policeman said. He was in his twenties, red-faced, grey-eyed, healthy-looking. 'My God, what swine! They'll do anything to drive these girls out, won't they? *Anything.*'

'It certainly looks like it,' agreed Rollison. 'Have you advised the Yard?'

'No. I just came to see——' the man hesitated, then took his transmitter out of the inside of his tunic. 'I'll report to the station, sir.'

'Yes. And someone must have seen this chap,' Rollison pointed out. 'He had to walk to the net, cut it, and walk back. Didn't you have a man out here?'

The policeman did not appear to be listening, but was reporting over the microphone.

'Edwards here, sir . . . Someone cut a hole in . . .'

Rollison moved off, leaving him to it. Two girls, one a flaxen-haired beauty who seemed to have stepped straight out of a film set, and a smaller one, with flaming red hair, were talking together. They stopped as Rollison came up with them, and fell into step by his side.

'Do you know who did it?' the taller girl asked.

'Not yet,' said Rollison.

'You never will,' said the red-head. 'Thank God *my* offspring was adopted last month, I don't have to stay any longer. It's a pretty foul situation, isn't it, Mr. Rollison?'

'Sickening,' responded Rollison. 'Apart from guesswork, do either of you know who is behind it all?'

Both of them looked up at Slatter's window; he was just turning away. Rollison went across to Anne, who was watching her companion crooning over a baby, obviously soothing herself as much as the child. Anne saw Rollison, and turned her head to him.

'Has he admitted it?' she asked drily.

'No,' answered Rollison.

'And no doubt you believe him,' Anne said stonily. 'This is about the last straw. Heaven knows what would have happened if Judy hadn't come out to see what was upsetting the babies.' She saw Rollison's expression, and went on: 'Yes, this is Judy Lyons.'

Judy half-turned.

'Hallo,' she said. She had a pert, pretty face and a bright, easy voice. 'I suppose you still think you're the great detective. After this, you don't imagine that any of us will buy that, do you?' She kept moving the child to-and-fro. 'I was one of those who said our worries were over when I heard you were interested, but I couldn't have been more wrong.' She tossed her head and turned back to Anne. 'What are we going to do?'

'We're going to cover up that hole,' Anne said, proving that she had been on the alert, 'and then we're going to have a rota watch while the babies are out here. We've three with chicken pox, and one of the mothers is down with it, too. And then—well, we'd better have a meeting this evening, to decide what to do. Will you come and answer some questions? On how the rats invaded the children of the damned?'

She, too, looked up at the window where Sir Douglas Slatter had been standing. But it was empty, now, and closed.

CHAPTER 14

MOTIVE

'Yes,' answered Rollison, 'I will come to the meeting if you'll give me safe conduct from angry mothers! What are you going to use to mend that wire?'

'I expect we'll use wire,' answered Anne. 'I know we promiscuous young women are not supposed to know about anything but luring young men to our beds, but we're very capable, really. Jennifer will—why, there *is* Jennifer!' A little girl who looked in her mid-teens appeared from the back door with a grey metal tool box in her hand, and a coil of wire over her shoulder. She had mousey hair and a snub nose and freckles beyond count, and was dressed in blue jeans and a loose fitting red shirt. She flashed brilliant green eyes at Rollison and Anne. 'Come and meet Mr. Rollison,' called Anne, and the child came across and dropped a mock curtsey.

'Good afternoon, Mr. Rollison, I've heard about you. Fancy actually admitting we exist!'

'And fancy you existing,' retorted Rollison. 'So you're the do-it-yourself member of the establishment?'

'When I wear trousers I'm the maintenance engineer,' said Jennifer. 'Do you know who made that hole?'

'No.'

'Well, as the great detective, why don't you find out what was happening next door?' suggested Jennifer. 'Anyone can sneak in from there and if your arms are long enough you

could actually stand in Sir D's garden and cut the wire. Or is he too rich to be suspected?'

'Jennifer, pet, the chips on your shoulders would make a log fire big enough to roast the poor devil,' protested Rollison. 'Haven't any of you heard of a little thing like evidence?'

She made a face at him, and walked past. The noise had subsided, and although there was much talk and now and again a subdued outburst of laughter, there was not a single crying baby.

'What time is your meeting?' asked Rollison.

'It'll be about half-past eight. You don't *have* to come,' Anne said. She turned her brown, speculative, almost brooding eyes towards him, and added: 'You don't always have to take me too seriously, either.'

'No,' agreed Rollison, 'but the choice is a little tricky. I can't always decide when you're telling the truth and when you're set on deceiving me.'

Once again he succeeded in shaking Anne Miller out of her calm. He smiled and turned. There was no sign of Naomi Smith, and had she been at home she would certainly have been here. He went through the house, heard a baby gurgling in a room on the right, but did not go in. A police car was in the street, and three plainclothes men were heading for the back of the house. Rollison recognised none of them, and did not stop. He turned again into Slatter's house, and rang the front door bell, as he had before.

Guy Slatter opened the door.

'Hallo,' he said, standing aside. 'Come in.' His manner showed a complete change from the aggressiveness of their last encounter. 'This time, I think, my uncle would like to see you.' He led the way upstairs, and as they reached the door of the study, Angela appeared at the end of the passage. Rollison glanced at young Slatter. He was surprised to catch on his face an expression of almost fatuous admiration.

Angela, looking very demure, gave a half-smile as she passed.

'Good afternoon, sir.'

Guy murmured something, as he opened Slatter's door. The most noticeable thing here, Rollison thought, was the quiet, although the window had been re-opened. Slatter placed a hand on some papers, to stop them from blowing, and rose from the desk.

I'm glad you came back,' he said. 'Please sit down. All right, Guy.'

Guy moved off with alacrity, letting the door close with a loud click. The old man looked across at it with resignation, but made no comment.

"Why *did* you come back?" he asked.

'To find out whether, after the rat interlude, you would reconsider your decision,' Rollison said. 'Obviously someone is determined to drive those girls away—by frightening them or pressuring them by threats of, and even by actual, murder. If you changed your mind, no one would retain the slightest suspicion that you are responsible.'

'Mr. Rollison,' said Slatter, placing both hands palms downwards on his desk, and looking like a newly-shaven Old Testament prophet, 'I shall not extend the tenancy of this house next door to those particular tenants. I am quite determined. I want peaceful occupancy of my own home and it is impossible in the present circumstances. They must go. However, the rat interlude, as you call it, did distress me. So did the attack on Mrs. Smith. I am not of course involved in either, and am quite indifferent to any form of suspicion which may fall on me, and your quite unworthy attempt to blackmail me into giving way is not the reason for what I am about to offer. I have a great deal of property in London, some in areas more suitable than this for a hostel. I am prepared to *give* premises of similar size to the sponsors of Smith Hall, on two conditions. One: that they move immediately the alternative accommodation is available, which I think will be very shortly. The other, that the transaction is kept quite confidential. No one is to know. And if you wonder why I make the second condition, I will tell you: if it were once known that I had made a gift I would be inundated with requests from other sources for donations.'

Rollison thought swiftly. A property of size anywhere in London would cost at least twenty thousand pounds, and such a gift even from a wealthy man was munificent indeed.

As he sat there, trying to think how best he could tell this man how warmly he regarded the offer, there was a violent crash, and a half-brick hurtling through the window. Startled by the expression on Rollison's face, which appeared a half-second before the impact, Slatter swivelled round in his chair.

'Duck!' roared Rollison.

But it was too late. Glass cascaded into the room, over Slatter's face and hands, over the desk and the floor. Rollison sprang to his feet. A sliver of glass cut into his cheek, causing sharp pain, but it did not stop him. He reached the window and peered out through the huge star-shaped hole in the glass.

No one was in sight. And the only place for anyone to hide was in the house next door.

He saw a policeman, running and staring up; he pointed to Smith Hall, then turned to face Sir Douglas Slatter.

Slatter was sitting, as if stunned, blood streaming down his face, where glass had struck the flesh like daggers.

In a sharp, authoritative voice, Rollison said: 'Sit still, Slatter. Just sit absolutely still.'

He glanced quickly outside again and saw Naomi Smith, then he turned back to the injured man. With gentle speed he pulled out the glass splinters—those from near the eye first. The astonishing thing was Slatter's statue-like stillness. His face was set, he did not move a muscle.

There were cries in the gardens outside, and a baby began to scream. There were also sounds inside this house, and as Rollison drew out the last splinter, the door opened and first Angela and then Naomi Smith appeared. Angela drew in her breath with a sharp hiss, Naomi's cheeks blanched but she came across without hesitation, and called to Angela:

'Bring a wet towel—quickly. Then a bowl and more towels.'

Angela turned and ran, as Rollison took out a handkerchief and placed it gently over the largest of the cuts.

'Unless your eye is damaged, there's nothing serious,' he said in a reassuring voice. He withdrew the handkerchief, now stained crimson, and went on: 'Open your eye slowly—very slowly.'

109

Slatter made no attempt to open his eye and did not move; it was almost impossible to detect the signs of breathing.

'Douglas,' Naomi said firmly and clearly, 'try to open your eyes.'

Her words had not the slightest effect, and she gave Rollison a quick, frightened glance. Rollison now saw a faint movement at Slatter's lips, and felt his pulse; it was beating very slowly. The eye was filling up with blood again and he dabbed the handkerchief on with great care.

'I think he's in shock,' he said. 'Do you know his doctor?'

'Yes—Dr. Morrison, who lives at Number 7.'

'Will you find out if he's in?'

'But——'

'I'll see to Sir Douglas,' Rollison promised.

She moved to the telephone as Angela came in with a towel, wrung out loosely. She unfolded it as she approached, then placed it with great care over Slatter's face. She did not press hard, but moulded it over his features, even into his eyes. Rollison had a moment to glance outside; a policeman was looking up at the window, as if measuring the distance.

'Is Dr. Morrison in?' Naomi sounded remarkably collected. 'Mrs. Smith, for Sir Douglas Slatter.'

Another policeman appeared inside the cage next door.

'We'll need more towels,' Rollison said to Angela. 'Is Guy Slatter in?'

'He went out five minutes before the—the crash.'

'All right,' said Rollison. 'Hurry with those towels.'

Naomi put the telephone down, saying with relief:

'We were lucky—he's coming at once.'

The cuts were bleeding less freely now, and had obviously been superficial. The alarming thing was Slatter's uncanny stillness.

'Naomi,' Rollison said, 'do you know who threw the brick?'

'I—I've no idea.'

'It must have been someone next door.'

'I can't believe any of the girls——' began Naomi, only to stop and close her eyes as if the very thought was painful. 'They—they said such wild things, I hardly knew what to think.'

'After the visitation by rats?'

'Yes. Mr. Rollison, who *is* doing these terrible things?'

'We're finding out,' answered Rollison grimly. 'But your job is to find out whether one of the girls threw this brick—and if one did, who it was.'

'But you said you were *sure* it came from Smith Hall.'

'Someone else could have gone in,' Rollison pointed out. He glanced outside again and saw one of the policemen beckoning—and at the same moment, Angela appeared with fresh towels. He drew back, watching Slatter, who still showed no sign of life but sat like a statue. 'I'll be back soon,' Rollison went on. 'We simply must find out if it was one of the girls.'

He went out and down the stairs. As he left by the front door, an old Rolls Royce pulled up and a middle-aged man got out, carrying a black bag. They met half-way along the drive.

'Dr. Morrison?'

'Yes.'

'You'll find the patient in his study.'

'Not alone, I trust!'

'No, not alone.'

'Are you—Mr. Rollison?'

'Yes,' said Rollison. He gave a brief, bleak smile, and then went—for once—out of this gateway into the next.

Standing in the window of Naomi Smith's room were Anne Miller and Judy Lyons; Judy was talking loudly and flinging her arms about, but the moment she saw Rollison, she stopped. Anne stared at him, as if in defiance. He did not go into the house but walked alongside it, to the two policemen. Almost as Rollison stopped in front of them a car pulled up in the street, and, glancing over his shoulder, Rollison saw three plainclothes policemen get out.

'Did you see who threw the brick?' asked Rollison.

'Yes,' one of the policemen said, with complete certainty. He smiled drily as he went on: 'You didn't expect that, did you, Mr. Rollison?'

'I hoped for it,' Rollison said mildly, but in fact he was astonished—it seemed almost too easy in this complex series of crimes. 'Who was it?'

'The tall, dark girl.'

'Anne Miller?'

'Anne, yes. I don't know her other name. Was Sir Douglas hurt?'

'Not badly, I hope,' Rollison said. 'A doctor's with him now.' He turned away and walked back briskly, meeting the plainclothes men near the porch.

As he entered the house, he heard Judy cry: 'It's no use, you've got to run away! They *saw* you, I know they saw you.'

'You're absolutely right,' Rollison said, pushing open the door of Naomi's room. 'They saw and can identify you, Anne —and if Sir Douglas should lose the sight of one eye, God knows what sentence the court would give you.'

'Oh, dear God!' gasped Judy.

Anne's eyes were narrowed but she did not move.

'You're trying to frighten me,' she said.

'I'm telling you that you're in real trouble,' Rollison said, 'and the fact that you felt viciously angry because of the rats won't be much help to you in court. Nor will you be able to pretend you didn't know that Sir Douglas was there, he could be seen from every window on this side of the house.' He swung round on Judy. 'Did Mrs. Smith give you a letter to post to me, two or three days ago?'

Judy shifted evasively, and mumbled, 'Yes.'

'Why didn't you post it?'

'But I did! I swear I did!'

'Judy, pet,' said Anne Miller, 'didn't you know that the great Richard Rollison can detect a lie before it actually passes your lips? Can't you, Mr. Rollison? The truth—as you appear to be so fond of it—is this. Judy asked *me* to post the letter and I promised her I would, but I did not. I will tell you another truth. I wanted to see what Mrs. Smith said to you, and steamed open the letter. I didn't like what it said, so I didn't send it.'

'What didn't you like?' asked Rollison.

'That I will not tell you,' Anne said.

'You can tell me instead, why you lied when you told Naomi Smith that Angela wanted to see her at Lyons Corner House,' said Rollison sharply.

'I suspected that Angela was a spy,' said Anne, simply. 'And when Mrs. Smith just rushed out, I knew I was right.'

As she finished, footsteps sounded in the hall and a man called out in a deep and authoritative voice:

'Is Miss Anne Miller in there, please?'

'Oh, Anne, Anne!' sobbed Judy. 'You should have run away!'

CHAPTER 15

HELP FROM GWENDOLINE

No one seemed less likely to run away than Anne Miller. She squeezed Judy's arm, then went to the door and opened it to two of the C.I.D. men who had just arrived. She stood aside, saying:

'I am Miss Anne Miller.'

'Thank you, Miss Miller.' The spokesman of the two was short, thickset, very fair-haired—almost an albino, with stubby eyelashes and colourless eyebrows. 'I am Detective Sergeant Adams of the Metropolitan Police.' His pale blue eyes flickered towards the Toff. 'Did you throw a brick at the first floor window of the house next door?'

Before anyone could speak or the Toff advise, Anne said:

'I did, with relish.'

'Are you aware of the gravity of your statement, Miss Miller?'

'I know what it means,' Anne answered.

'I have to inform my superiors, Miss Miller. May I have your assurance that you will remain here to answer further questions?'

'And supposing I won't promise?' asked Anne.

'Oh, *Anne,*' breathed Judy Lyons. 'Oh, think what you've done.'

'Then on evidence available I should have to charge you with an offence and take you to Scotland Yard or to the nearest Divisional Headquarters.'

'I have a defenceless baby here, Sergeant,' Anne said, silkily.

'All necessary arrangements would be made, Miss Miller.' Again the Sergeant's gaze flickered towards the Toff. 'I am quite sure Mr. Rollison would advise——'

'I am quite capable of making my own decisions,' Anne said, coldly. 'I will stay here.'

'I hope you will have no cause to regret your decision,' said Sergeant Adams, with a formality which Rollison had not heard from a policeman for a long time. 'Good afternoon, Miss.' He nodded to Rollison. 'Good afternoon, Mr. Rollison.' He moved towards the door, hesitated, and then turned back. 'Were you a witness to the brick-throwing, sir?'

'I didn't see it leave,' answered Rollison drily. 'I saw it arrive.'

'Did you see the injury caused to Sir Douglas Slatter, sir?'

'Yes.'

'In all likelihood, sir, a statement will shortly be required of you. Will you undertake to be——'

'I'll be in London,' promised Rollison briskly. 'Anne, don't make any more admissions, but do make preparations for being away for a few days. Will one of the others look after your baby?'

'Oh, I will!' cried Judy.

'Yes,' said Anne. 'I shall be perfectly all right. But I may not be at the meeting tonight,' she added with a touch of bitterness.

Rollison looked at her for what seemed a long time, and then he moved towards the door, saying: 'I don't know whether you're very good or very bad, but I do know you're a remarkable young woman.' He reached the door with one of his unbelievably swift movements, slipping past the two detectives as if he were a wraith; once out of the house he walked swiftly towards his car, and drove off. He was watched by two policemen and the detectives, and he caught a glimpse of Angela on the doorstep of Slatter's house; the doctor's vintage Rolls Royce was still outside.

Twenty minutes later, Rollison turned into a narrow lane off Fleet Street, parking his car half on the roadway and half

115

on the pavement. Striding along a narrow alley, which had run between two buildings for at least a hundred and fifty years, he came to a modern plaza from which rose a vast edifice of cement and glass, dwarfing the ancient buildings nearby.

This was the new house of The Globe Newspapers Limited.

If he had any luck, Gwendoline Fell would be in her office.

She was indeed, an unbelievable Gwendoline Fell, wearing a huge, floppy-brimmed flowered hat, a sleeveless dress of a delicate shade of puce, and elbow length kid gloves; and she was ravishingly made-up. Four girls and a long-haired youth sat in an outer office reading newspapers, two of them cutting out columns and articles with huge, shiny shears. Each looked up at the Toff with unashamed curiosity; and each manoeuvred to get a better look at him as he shook hands with Gwendoline.

'Do sit down,' she said.

'Where do you keep your motor-scooter?' he inquired.

'Near enough to give me no difficulty in following shady individuals,' answered Gwendoline Fell, half-smiling. 'What trouble can I help to get you out of, Mr. Rollison? Or perhaps I should ask if you've come to plead with me not to make a big story out of your latest abysmal failure. Do you feel proud to have been sitting with poor Sir Douglas when the glass splintered in his face? And how clever you were—only two small scratches yourself, I see.'

'Ah,' said Rollison. 'But I lead the charmed life of the indolent and the lucky.' He gave his gayest smile. 'Do you want to find out the truth about the vendetta against Naomi Smith and her fallen angels?'

'Her—*what*? Oh, I see. Your name for them. How very poetical. If I were in an argumentative mood I might toss up whether to challenge the first part of it or the second. But please go on.' She smiled, suddenly all charm.

'You're very kind,' said Rollison drily. 'I now doubt very much if Sir Douglas Slatter is the villain, which means that I think someone else is engineering the hate campaign. If it is believed that Sir Douglas has given in and is allowing the girls

116

to stay in Number 31, the campaign to drive them out will be stepped up, and——'

'You *are* on the side of the fallen angels,' interrupted Gwendoline. 'Do you want them all to have their heads bashed in?'

Rollison sat back in his chair and looked at her levelly, then slowly rose to his feet and turned away. He did not hurry, neither did he dawdle. He could just see the outline of Gwendoline's face and hat in one of the glass walls turned into a mirror by two filing cabinets, and beyond he saw the occupants of the outer office trying to disguise their interest. Gwendoline neither moved nor spoke, even when he opened the door. She believed he would turn back, of course, that he was merely bluffing. He nodded pleasantly to the others and went into the glass-walled passage beyond, without once looking back. As last he came upon a wall through which he could not see; beyond was the battery of lifts, and a clock made in the shape of a map of the earth with the words 7*th Floor* above it.

He pressed for a lift, to go down. He was not angry, not even annoyed, and only slightly exasperated; he simply did not see how any good could come of such persistent conflict; and as Gwendoline had not come after him or sent one of her staff, she was apparently in no mood to change. It was a pity, but he had friends in Fleet Street who would undoubtedly give this case the kind of publicity he believed it required.

The automatic lift was some time in arriving. He was the only occupant, and as he strode through the hall he met only messenger girls and doormen. He stepped on to the plaza of near-dazzling white steps, opposite the alley, and turned towards the narrow entrance. As he did so, a motor-scooter engine pop-pop-popped from the right, and round a corner of *The Globe* building came Gwendoline Fell in all her finery, including the hat, astride her motor-scooter. Rollison stopped, and she drew level with him.

'Please come back,' she pleaded. 'I won't be bitchy again.'

He looked at the absurd hat, and his determination wavered.

He could impose conditions; he could complain or explain

or ask her to listen to reason. Instead, he found himself smiling.

'Whatever you are, you'll be. But yes, I'll come back. Shall I come with you, or——'

Gwendoline gave the stand of the scooter a most unladylike kick, and got off. She raised a hand to one of *The Globe* employees. 'George will look after this, won't you George,' she said, then strode along at Rollison's side, back to the building.

None of her staff looked up this time; only their scissors seemed to snip with very much greater vigour. Inside the main office, Gwendoline went back to her chair, tapping the arm of Rollison's as she passed it.

'How can I help?' she asked.

'Tell the world in your column tomorrow that Sir Douglas has a heart of gold and you have it on good authority that he has given way to the angels, who may stay in possession of the house.'

'Has he?' asked Gwendoline.

'Can I speak strictly off the record?'

'Yes.'

'He is not going to renew the lease of Smith Hall but he *is* going to give them another house.'

'*Give?*' echoed Gwendoline, her eyes rounding.

'Give,' repeated Rollison solemnly.

'And I can't say *that?*' sighed Gwendoline. 'I *am* only flesh and blood, you know.'

'He told me in strict confidence. And even if he hadn't, I wouldn't want you to use the full facts yet. Isn't the truth enough to make your story sensational? Before the rat incident he was adamantly hostile, so he had a remarkable change of heart.'

'He certainly did,' agreed Gwendoline. 'Can you be sure that if I tell the story, as you ask me to, it will get the results you want?'

'I'm sure there's a good chance of it doing so. I think there will be more attacks, but that house and those girls will be as closely protected as royalty. I don't believe, this time, there

118

will be the slightest chance of the attackers either doing harm or getting away.'

They sat quite still, their eyes meeting in a silent challenge. At last Gwendoline gave a decisive little nod.

'I'll do it your way,' she said. 'May I add one plea?'

'Yes, of course.'

'Can I know what help you're going to get?'

Rollison chuckled.

'Yes, gladly. Meet me at ten o'clock tonight outside the entrance to Aldgate East Underground Station, crash helmet, motor-scooter and all.'

'I'll be there,' said Gwendoline with relish. 'I will certainly be there! Is there anything else I can do to help?'

'At this moment, check at the Yard to see if Superintendent Grice is in and if he'll see me right away,' said Rollison.

Before he had finished speaking she was lifting the telephone, and he listened as she spoke crisply and precisely: at the desk she seemed much more mature. She replaced the receiver, and nodded with satisfaction.

'I understand that he wants to see you,' she said, and this time the glint in her eyes was mischievous. 'I hope you'll be free to meet me tonight.'

Grice was in his bright new office at the bright new building which would never, for Rollison, capture the romantic appeal of the old Scotland Yard. About a quarter of the size of Gwendoline Fell's, there was all glass in one wall. The others, decently opaque, were hung with photographs of police football and cricket teams, and long-pensioned-off senior officers. Grice motioned to a chair.

'What's the latest news about Slatter?' Rollison asked.

'He's now at the Moorfields Eye Hospital,' answered Grice. 'They're checking for glass splinters. He's still in a state of traumatic shock, and it could last for days. I'm told you were present when the Miller girl admitted throwing the brick.'

'I was,' said Rollison. 'I was also there when the brick came through the window, and if I hadn't shown how alarmed I was, Slatter wouldn't have looked round—and then all he

119

would have got would have been splinters of glass in his scalp. With hair as thick as his I doubt if that would have amounted to much more than a few scratches. Are you going to charge Anne Miller?'

'Yes—I've no choice. I'm going to pick her up this evening, after she's finished her motherly chores, and ask for the case to be heard early in the morning,' Grice answered. 'And I shan't oppose bail. That will give you a week to find a way of getting her off!' Grice spoke almost bitterly. 'Do you yet know what's behind it all?'

'I only wish I did,' Rollison said, 'I was hoping you would have an idea. Do you know anything more about the rats in the children's pen?'

'No.'

'No trace of the assailant?'

'None.'

'No clues as to the deaths of Brown and Webberson and the two girls?'

Grice hesitated, and then said: 'Well, yes and no. It's beginning to look as if they knew both Winifred de Vaux and Iris Jay a little more intimately than is usual between professor and pupil.'

'Hmm. Do you know if any of the other girls were associated with any of the sponsors?'

'As far as I've been able to trace, none at all. Nimmo is married and has a very good reputation, Carfax is incapacitated because of his paralysis, and Offenberger is courting an Austrian woman who keeps house for him. But I've no evidence at all to show why Brown and Webberson should be killed, or why Mrs. Smith should have been attacked. One obvious possibility is that they all shared some knowledge which the murderer doesn't want divulged. Has Mrs. Smith given you any hint?'

'No,' answered Rollison, truthfully.

'Have you turned anything up?' Grice asked.

'No,' said Rollison again. 'All I know is——' he told Grice all he could, including what he had arranged with Gwendoline Fell, and he told him of Slatter's offer of a house. Then he left, a little after half-past five, with only one thought in mind.

He needed a talk with Naomi Smith, who might know more, much more, than she had yet admitted.

CHAPTER 16

'NO,' SAYS NAOMI SMITH

'No,' said Naomi flatly. 'I know absolutely nothing more than I've told you.' She looked so earnest and so plain, so homely and so wholesome; throughout the crisis she had maintained her outward composure remarkably. Now, her make-up was fresh, with just enough lipstick to make the best of her full lips, and she had a scarcely discernible shade of eye-shadow, so that her chestnut brown eyes seemed to have a slight sheen over them.

Rollison thought of Slatter's injured eye.

'Naomi,' Rollison said, almost harshly, 'if you are protecting someone——'

'But I am not,' she insisted. Her voice had a tone of restrained indignation. 'How can you think that I would allow such terrible things to happen in order to protect any individual? It is unthinkable. Four—four of my *friends*, brutally murdered. Sir Douglas perhaps blinded—*no*, Mr. Rollison, I know nothing that could help. I am at the edge of a dreadful precipice. All I have fought for and believed in, all I have tried to do, is faced with absolute disaster. If I knew a thing —if I had the slightest suspicion against any individual—I would tell you. But I know nothing.'

Without a pause, Rollison asked: 'Did you know that Keith Webberson was friendly with Winifred de Vaux?—so friendly, in fact, that he had a large photograph of her displayed in his flat? And that Professor Brown——'

She looked at him furiously. 'How knowledge of these girls' misfortune distorts everything they do! Is no man to be their friend without the grossest interpretation being put on it?' Alarm added to the brightness of her eyes, and her lips trembled.

'Do—do the police think as you do?'

Rollison shrugged.

'Will it be made public?'

'Whether some bright newspaperman will find it out and tell the story, I don't know. It wouldn't be surprising.'

'No,' she said in a low-pitched voice. 'Obviously it would be exactly the kind of scandal the newspapers would glory in. And that *does* mean the end of this house and all I've tried to do. You must see that in a place like this, rumour that it is little more than a brothel and I the madame, are always possible. However dormant the suggestion, it is there, ready at the slightest excuse to be taken up by a certain section of society. And Douglas warned——' She broke off, and closed her eyes as if suffering from a spasm of acute pain.

The 'Douglas' came out with unexpected familiarity, strangely at variance with the formality of her previous references to Slatter.

'What did Sir Douglas warn you about?' asked Rollison gently.

'That the house and I would get this reputation,' she said, opening her eyes. 'We are old friends, Mr. Rollison, although until I came here we hadn't met for many years. When I first knew that he owned this house I went to see him, asking for his help—but he had no sympathy at all with what I was trying to do. He was furiously angry because he had signed the lease without being told what it was going to be used for. It—it was not a very pleasant meeting,' Naomi finished, on a note both saddening and dreary.

'How often have you met since?'

'Only occasionally.'

'Socially?'

'Once or twice. He—he is a very good man, Mr. Rollison, and he did not believe that because we differed fundamentally on this aspect of society—I have always believed that

123

unmarried mothers and illegitimate children should be given special consideration, because of what they inevitably miss, having no husband, and no father—we should not remain friends.' She raised her hands and dropped them again. 'Douglas maintained that if you broke the rules of the society you lived in, you should accept the consequence. I can see his point of view, of course.' Unexpectedly, her voice sharpened. 'Can *you*, Mr. Rollison?'

'I can see both points of view,' parried Rollison.

'A friend to both sides is said to be a friend to none,' Naomi said a little bitterly. 'Nevertheless, I still need your help. Mr. Rollison, can you help Anne? I know she shouldn't have done what she did but it *was* under terrible provocation, and I am sure she hadn't the slightest intention of injuring Douglas.'

'I can get a good lawyer to speak for her and ask for bail,' said Rollison.

'Oh, if only you will!'

'I'll have a word with Professor Nimmo and make sure I'm not treading on any corns,' promised Rollison. 'Are the girls going to meet together tonight?'

'Yes,' said Noami, and caught her breath. 'I think at least half of them will leave at once.' She gave herself a little shake and rose to her feet. Her movements and her manner had become more decisive, as if for the moment, at least, she had done with brooding and with being sorry for herself. 'I'm very grateful for all you are doing. Will you come this evening?'

'If I may.'

'I don't think you can do anything to help them,' said Naomi, 'but you will at least see and understand the mood of the girls. It's so very sad,' she went on, in her brisker voice, 'only a few weeks ago everything appeared to be going so well.' She led the way to the door, and then touched the back of his hand. 'Mr. Rollison, please understand and believe one thing. Professor Webberson and Dr. Brown did not take advantage of their position as sponsors. There was a very real friendship in both cases.'

124

Friendship, love, or simply lust, thought Rollison grimly, neither men had deserved to be murdered; nor had either of the girls.

And now Naomi Smith was telling the truth, which he wanted and hoped to be the case, or she was a consummate liar.

As he walked to his car, parked further away this time, he saw Guy Slatter walking towards him. He stopped as Guy drew up, aware of the powerful physique and the rugged good looks of the young man, who was so like his uncle.

'How is Sir Douglas?' Rollison asked.

'I'm assured there's no permanent damage to the eyes,' said Guy, harshly. 'No thanks to you. *Now* do you think those little bitches are worth protecting? If I had my way I'd send 'em all to a whore-house!'

'You know,' said Rollison, 'that doesn't do you any credit.'

'If you're still on the side of that mob, you're a bloody fool,' growled Guy. 'You do-gooders make me sick!' He strode past, head held high, and Rollison walked more slowly towards his car. As he drew near, he thought he saw a shadowy movement in the back. All thought of the Slatters and the girls vanished. If someone was in the back of his car, it meant trouble—and a single sledge hammer blow would put an end to his interest in crime forever. He glanced down as he drew close, and saw a rug move. He opened the driving door, but instead of getting in he simply leaned inside, and said roughly:

'Put that rug off you, and show your hands. And hurry!'

There was a convulsive movement—and then the rug was pushed off and two hands appeared; even he did not think there was the slightest chance that they were big enough to hold a sledge hammer. They were small and plump and very familiar.

'I don't want anyone to know I'm here,' breathed Angela. 'Guy came out to look for me. Just get in and pretend you're alone. We can talk when we're at Gresham Terrace or anywhere you want to take me. But please hurry,' she pleaded. 'I've something I'm desperately anxious to tell you. I think I may have solved the case!'

Rollison heard all this as he drew his head back, got into the car in the normal way, sat back and touched the wheel.

'You can tell me as we go along,' he ordered.

He pushed the self-starter—and on the first instant of pressure, the front of the car blew up.

One moment he had only the thought of Angela and what she had to say in his mind; the next, the metal of the bonnet bulged upwards and upwards, there was a vivid red flash and then leaping flames, and as the windscreen cracked into a thousand tiny fragments, a roar and a blast.

A few pieces of glass fell over his knees.

The car rocked, as wildly as if it were a small boat in high seas. The flames rose higher and dark smoke billowed, and through the smoke Rollison saw a man reeling back, hand over his eyes, and he had a fierce and frightening recollection of Sir Douglas Slatter's cut and bleeding face. But he could not move; in those few seconds he was too shocked and numbed. He saw other figures, men and women, hurrying towards the reeling man, was aware of cars pulled up in the road, saw a man leap from one with a small fire-extinguisher in his hand.

The sight seemed to revive Rollison. He pulled his own extinguisher from its clips beside the brake, and turned to look at Angela, suddenly alarmed lest she was hurt. She looked more startled than scared, her eyes and mouth open wide and round. He opened his door and jumped out, opened her door and said: 'Get out, quick!' and strode to the front of the car. The bent and broken bonnet was now a mass of foam, there was an evil stench of the chemical and a smell also of burning. But the flames were out, and a little man with the remains of a huge cigar still jutting out beneath his hooked nose, was lowering his extinguisher.

'I got it,' he said with satisfaction.

'I can't even begin to thank you,' Rollison said, looking towards the once reeling man who was standing in the middle of a small group.

'Who wants thanks?' the Good Samaritan said. 'You'd do the same for me. You okay, sir?'

'I'm—yes, thanks. I'm fine. I hope——'

'You in a hurry to go any place? I'll be glad to take you.'

'I'd better wait for the police to come here,' said Rollison, 'but if you could take my passenger——'

'Sure, sure, be glad to,' the cigar-smoker said. 'That's if *you're* okay, Miss.'

It was not until Angela was being driven away in a sky-blue Jaguar that Rollison wondered whether he should have let her go, whether the helpful motorist could possibly have known who had put the explosive in the car. It was too late to stop her, and a police car was already pulling up, while a policeman was standing in the road, urging the traffic on. Very little had been tossed into the air, the metal of the bonnet was too strong. The man nearest the explosion had covered his face in time to escape the full effect of a billow of steam from the burst radiator, and was comparatively unhurt.

The engine, which had taken the full force of the explosion, was wrecked. Oil was dripping out of the sump, and there was a strong smell of petrol.

Wired to the base of the self-starter was a scrap of red cardboard.

'So they used dynamite,' remarked a policeman. It was the fair-haired Detective Sergeant Adams, who had seen Anne Miller. He shook his head lugubriously. 'A chance in a million, Mr. Rollison, that you're not in hospital by now.'

'If not in a morgue,' added Rollison lightly. 'Sergeant, need I stay? I didn't see who put it there, but you may find a passer-by who noticed someone. May I leave the rest to you?'

'You *have* been in touch with Mr. Grice of the Yard, sir, haven't you?'

'I saw him only an hour ago.'

'And where can we find you, sir?'

Rollison gave him the Gresham Terrace address, then espied a taxi putting down a passenger a few houses along the street. Pushing through the crowd he ran towards it. It was not until he sat back, heavily, that the shock waves struck him. For a few moments he was very cold and shivery, and his forehead and upper lip were beaded with sweat. He was halfway towards Gresham Terrace before he began to feel acute anxiety for Angela. What on earth had possessed him, to allow her to go off with a stranger?

Turning out of the far end of Gresham Terrace as his cab turned in at the end nearer Piccadilly, was a sky-blue Jaguar. Relief surged over him.

Waiting for him at the open door of his flat were Jolly and Angela—Angela holding a glass of brandy. She looked pale and shaken, but her voice was calm enough. Jolly, very solicitous, ushered him to his favourite armchair, and brought him whisky and a soda-syphon.

'As Miss Angela said you weren't likely to be long, I've timed dinner for seven-fifteen, sir,' he said. 'And Miss Angela will be staying.'

'If that's all right with you, Uncle Richard,' Angela said demurely.

Rollison looked at her anxiously. She had a tiny cut on her right temple, where blood had dried, and a reddish bruise on her left cheek.

'What makes you think you've solved the case?' he asked.

She did not answer at once, but sniffed the bouquet from the large glass.

He wondered if he should have given her more time to recover, whether she was really in a condition to answer and to think. Then he reminded himself that she was very tough indeed, as well as highly intelligent. He did not press her, but waited, sipping his whisky, grateful in a perverse way for her prolonged silence.

At last, she said: 'I don't really think there's any doubt, Rolly. Sir Douglas himself is behind it all. Look what I found in a drawer in his wardrobe.'

She opened her handbag and took out three nylon stockings, all full of runs and all odd-shaped, as if they had been used to adorn something very different indeed from a leg; it was easy to imagine that they had been pulled over a man's face and had lost their shape. As Rollison fingered the stockings, Angela dipped again into her handbag, and this time drew out a pair of big, dark blue cotton gloves—the kind of gloves a man might wear if he wanted to grip a handle tightly, yet was anxious not to leave fingerprints.

128

Angela was looking eagerly into Rollison's face, waiting for his approval. He smiled at her thoughtfully, and asked:

'Was the drawer locked?'

'Yes, but I found his keys.'

'Where?' asked Rollison.

'In his trousers pocket,' answered Angela shamelessly. 'They undressed him before he was taken to the hospital, and I had to take care of his clothes. I couldn't fold them and put them away with everything in the pockets, could I?'

'Obviously not,' answered Rollison. 'Did you look anywhere else?'

'I wanted to, but as a matter of fact I got cold feet,' answered Angela, with engaging frankness. 'And Guy was a bit troublesome, too. You'd think he'd never seen an attractive young woman before—he says it's a case of love at first sight, and I must say he behaves almost as if he means it. As a matter of fact, I think he's rather nice.'

'I hope you're right,' said Rollison, looking at her thoughtfully. 'Is Sir Douglas coming home tonight?'

'No, he's being kept at the hospital for at least twenty-four hours. Why?'

'Do you think you could lure young Guy to take you to a night-club, or any place where you'll be out late?' asked Rollison. 'I'd very much like to have a look round at Number 29.'

'Well,' said Angela, after considering, 'I will certainly try, and I shouldn't think it would be too difficult. I——'

Two things happened simultaneously, to make her break off. The telephone bell rang, and Jolly appeared to say with customary solemnity that dinner was about to be served. Rollison got up and reached for the telephone while Angela finished her brandy with almost sacrilegious haste, and hurried out with a 'Three jiffs, Jolly.'

'This is Richard Rollison,' Rollison said.

'You've had a taste of what will happen to you if you don't keep out of Slatter's business,' a man said. His voice was muffled, as if he were speaking through gauze or muslin. *Or a nylon stocking*, thought Rollison. 'You keep out of it, or a lot more heads will be smashed in, including yours.'

CHAPTER 17

BUSY EVENING

As Rollison hung up, Angela appeared again, her bright hair brushed with school-girl precision. Jolly, who had also disappeared, returned with a laden tray. Obviously Rollison's expression told them both that this had not been a normal call.

'Anything to do with us?' inquired Angela.

'I trust there is no immediate emergency,' said Jolly.

'Just an Awful Warning of what will happen to me if I don't turn my back on the fallen angels,' said Rollison lightly, and went on almost in the same breath 'By George, I'm hungry!' He pulled a chair away from the table for Angela, and as they had dinner—lamb cutlets, green peas and new potatoes, all with rare flavour—he talked to Angela and recalled lunching here with Naomi Smith and the way she had introduced him to this case.

Jolly hovered, was praised for his cooking, and was duly gratified.

Angela left at half-past eight, promising to call the flat if she failed to lure Guy out of his uncle's house.

Rollison left at a quarter to nine, at the wheel of Jolly's ancient Austin A35, a small grey car which would be blown to smithereens if a stick of dynamite were wired to the self-starter. The streets were empty and it took only ten minutes to reach Bloomdale Street. There was a parking place quite near Smith Hall, and here, under the stern eye of a watchful policeman, he left his car. There were a lot of police about; he spotted at least four. So Grice had taken his extra precautions early.

'Good evening, sir,' one of them said. 'Are you all right? . . . Very nasty thing to happen, that explosion.'

'Yes, I'm fine. But make sure no one puts dynamite in this one, won't you?'

'Don't you worry, sir. We'll watch it like lynxes!'

Rollison murmured 'I'm sure you will,' and walked towards the house, recalling the shadowy figure of the bestockinged assailant on his first visit here. No-one threw a shadow tonight, but a policeman stood near the porch in the full light of a street lamp.

The door was closed, and Rollison rang the bell. After a brief pause, Judy Lyons appeared, still very subdued. She peered out nervously, then stood aside.

'We thought you weren't coming,' she said.

'I hope you're glad I have,' replied Rollison.

'I'm not sure that it makes any difference,' said Judy tartly. 'We're all upstairs, in the drawing-room.'

The room was immediately above Naomi Smith's study, but was much larger. Round the walls were couches and armchairs, other smaller chairs and tables with magazines were in the middle. In one corner stood an old radiogram, and by the side of it was a small table, at which Naomi was sitting. Rollison made a swift count of heads, and reached twenty-two. Anne Miller had not yet been taken to the police station; she sat with her long, slim legs stretched out, apparently deep in thought. The girls, all about the same age, were of all shapes and sizes, dark-haired and fair. There was one sad-faced Indian woman with the red spot on her forehead, showing that she was a Hindu of good caste, and one short, dumpy African girl with a very lively face.

Every eye was turned towards Rollison; one elfin little creature in pale green blew him a kiss.

Naomi pointed to an empty chair at her side.

"Please come and sit down, Mr. Rollison. We had just decided to wait until you came, in the hope that you could give us some encouraging news.'

131

'Not a hope in a thousand,' a girl said clearly.

'It's a waste of time,' chimed in another.

Naomi's eyes flashed, she rapped sharply on the table, calling them to attention.

'The very least you can do is show good manners!' she said icily.

Stung, Anne threw her head up, ready for argument. 'But Mr. Rollison's good manners didn't prevent him from being three-quarters of an hour late, Mrs. Smith. Perhaps a little bird told him that we can't be deceived any more, and that we've decided to leave here and make our own plans, instead of waiting to have our heads bashed in, or our babies bitten by rats. We've decided, too, that all these mysterious comings and goings are a waste of time, designed for the sole object of giving Mr. Rollison a sense of his own self-importance. Good manners will hardly disguise the fact that the promised miracle hasn't come off.' There was a break in the young, scornful voice, and Rollison bit back the sharp rejoinder which rose to his lips.

'You're all under great strain,' he said easily. 'And that's hardly surprising. The situation was bad enough when you had to come here; it's still a cold and conventional world and you broke the rules. What's happened now makes it ten times worse. Probably half of you think that some bigoted person is out to make you pay for it.' He paused long enough to look round at every face, let his gaze come to rest on Anne's, and then went on: 'I don't think this is true. I don't think these unfortunate people have been murdered in cold blood for the sake of a principle which is fairly loosely interpreted in this day and age. I think there is a very powerful material motive which no-one yet suspects. Whoever is behind these crimes stands to gain a great deal. I don't, as yet, know what, and I don't know who. I do know you can't stand it much longer. The situation is unbearable, and I think tomorrow will see the end of it.'

Several faces lit up.

'And I think the end may come when the criminals make one final tremendous effort to force you out of here,' Rollison went on. 'If you go, you'll be playing into their hands, if you stay you may be in very grave danger indeed.'

When he stopped, no-one spoke until Naomi asked in a very quiet voice

'What do you advise, Mr. Rollison?'

'I can't advise anything,' said Rollison. 'I hope you'll stay. If I'm right and it's all over by tomorrow——'

'We still have our marching orders from Slatter,' Anne remarked. 'We can't win.'

'If it's over by tomorrow,' said Rollison, quietly, 'I think there's an even chance that Sir Douglas will change his mind.'

'You mean there would have been if Anne hadn't thrown that brick,' said the African girl, simply, and without bitterness. 'You can't seriously believe that Sir Douglas would relent after that.'

'I seriously believe it,' Rollison assured her.

'I think we all ought to make preparations to leave,' Anne said. 'I——' She broke off as a bell rang sharp and clear, and suddenly her expression changed. Something like near-despair touched her. 'I have to anyhow. That will be the police. This is arrest by appointment,' she went on. 'They said they would come for me at half-past nine.'

Judy was staring at her helplessly.

'I have to go, too,' said Rollison. 'I'll come down with you.' Anne stood up, so tall and slim and strangely lonely and forlorn. 'And I'm absolutely serious,' he said to the others. 'I think tomorrow may be the last day.'

No-one spoke as he went out. Naomi jumped up, but he waved her back to her chair, and opened the door for Anne. There was a knock and a ring. He went ahead and opened the door cautiously, but this was no trick; there were three police officers in the porch, and the one in the middle was Adams.

'Miss Anne Miller?' he asked formally.

'Anne,' said Rollison, 'if you need help, you have only to ask me.'

He heard Naomi hurrying down the stairs, obviously to

133

offer what comfort she could. He nodded to the policemen and left the house.

There was no way of being sure the girls would stay on, but he believed they would. And if they did, and he was right in his supposition that tomorrow would see the whole hideous affair cleared up, then tomorrow would hold for them their greatest danger yet.

And he would have brought it upon them . . .

Two policemen watched him go.

Two policemen, obviously by coincidence, were standing outside Aldgate East Underground Station when he pulled up some distance away, and they were looking about them as if idly, but with particular interest at Gwendoline Fell, who stood by the side of her motor-scooter which was parked right outside the station. She looked questioningly at the policemen, then glanced round in Rollison's direction. Her eyes lit up. The policemen, too, glanced at Rollison as Gwendoline went hurrying towards him, eager now as if to a lover. Rollison took both her hands.

'I was half afraid you wouldn't get here,' she said, gripping tightly. 'Are you all right?' She searched his face. 'Don't look so innocent!' she cried. 'You *were* nearly blown-up, weren't you?'

'That story's got around, has it?' Rollison said, and laughed. 'Yes, I survived. I'm afraid the car I'm now using isn't big enough to put your motor-scooter in the boot.'

'I'll leave it here,' she said, and they turned and walked back to Jolly's battered Austin. She appeared not to notice its age and condition. 'You're going to get a front page headline in *The Globe*, and probably in other papers, too.'

'I don't deserve it,' Rollison said. 'Will it also be connected with Slatter?'

'Yes.'

'I hope to heaven I've done the right thing.'

'Let me be the judge of that,' said Gwendoline primly. 'Off the record.'

He told her what he expected and had asked, and added as he drove along Commercial Road:

'The police are already watching Smith Hall in strength,

but they will probably be recognised, and I want some strong-arm men who won't be. Have you ever heard of the Blue Dog?'

'In Wapping? Or is it Whitechapel?'

'Whitechapel,' Rollison said. 'So you've heard of it.' He turned two corners, and on the next was a public house, the woodwork painted bright blue, and the inn-sign yellow with a blue-painted mongrel. Several people went in and two came out as they passed. Rollison turned this corner, and on the left was a big wooden building, over the front of which ran the legend: *Ebbutt's Gym*. Some elderly men and a few youths stood about, the youths sparring. Rollison pulled up near the entrance, and a man called:

'Lumme! It's Mr. Ar!'

'Where's Bill?' called Rollison.

'In the pub, Mr. Ar!'

Rollison was giving Gwendoline Fell a hand.

'Ask him if he can spare me a few minutes here,' said Rollison.

'Sure will, Mr. Ar!' The man, small and with a nutcracker face, hurried towards the back of the Blue Dog. The youths stopped sparring, and stared with great interest at the Toff and his companion. The door of the gymnasium was open and the sound of leather on leather came clearly. Rollison pushed aside a canvas flap, remarking for all to hear:

'I'm bringing in a lady.'

'S'okay,' said another, smaller man in a white polo-necked sweater. 'Always welcome, Mr. Ar, with or without!' He beamed welcome at Gwendoline with a grin stretching from cauliflower ear to cauliflower ear.

The gymnasium was much bigger than it looked from outside. There were two boxing rings, both occupied by youngsters, half-a-dozen men gathered around each. The walls were fitted with parallel bars, there were vaulting horses and punch balls, everything, in fact, needed for training in a modern gymnasium. Over in one corner was a small office, partitioned off. In another was a door marked 'Showers'. The doorkeeper hovered near as Rollison explained.

'Bill Ebbutt, who owns this and runs the pub next door, used to be a heavyweight,' Rollison began.

'*And a bloody good un, too,*' interpolated the doorman.

'And he trains promising youngsters for nothing or next-to-nothing,' said Rollison.

'*Picks the good uns, too,*' whispered the doorman.

'And a lot of old professionals come in and help with the training. It's really a kind of club.'

'*And a good un, too,*' repeated the doorman. Then his voice rose: 'Here's Bill,' he announced with obvious pride, and waved a hand in greeting as Bill Ebbutt came in.

Ebbutt was huge, bald-headed, treble-chinned and wheezy of breath. He wore an enormous polo-necked sweater of a heather-mixture wool; knitting it must have been a year's labour of love. So big was his jowl and so comparatively small his head that he looked rather like one pear reared upon another. His eyes, deeply buried, were a bright, periwinkle blue.

'Cor lumme, Mr. Ar, you're a sight for sore eyes.' He engulfed Rollison's hand. 'Glad to see you, always will be, who's your lady friend?' He towered above Gwendoline, who looked up at him with barely-concealed amazement.

'Miss Gwendoline Fell,' said Rollison.

'Glad to meetcha, Miss Fell, any friend of Mr. Rollison's——' he extended a vast hand, but before he took Gwendoline's a change came over his expression, and almost in a whisper, he said: 'Not the bitch who writes in *The Globe*?' He raised both hands in an onslaught of horror. 'I never ought to 'ave said that, I'm sorry, I——'

'Very well put, Mr. Ebbutt,' said Gwendoline calmly. 'That's what at least half a million readers think of me.' She beamed up at him. 'I don't mind what I say about them, so why should I mind what they say about me?'

'I daresay,' said Bill, still abashed. 'All the same, I never ought to say things like that to a guest. Here! Not come to do a story about me and my boys, have you? I dunno that I want——'

'I just wanted her to know I'm not the nincompoop I sometimes look,' said Rollison. 'Can we go into the office?' They crowded in, while sparring and the vaulting, the punching and the jumping continued. 'Bill,' went on Rollison, 'I need about two dozen of your boys for a job which could be very nasty.' He explained, wasting no words, obviously confident that Bill Ebbutt did not need telling anything twice.

'I get the picture,' Ebbutt said. 'If anyone does lay on a kind of all-out attack, you don't want to be caught napping. What do you really want, Mr. Ar? One man for one girl? Only way to make sure they get absolute protection.'

'If you can manage to find twenty-two——'

'Cor, bless you, there's so much short time and redundancy I could do fifty! Get 'em over there asking for jobs, no one will be surprised. O.K., Mr. Ar, you leave it to me. The flipping coppers—beg your pardon, Miss—are the first line of attack, we stand by to pick up the pieces. I'll go over and spy out the land after the pub's closed. Now, how about coming across to the Blue Dog for a couple, Mr. Ar? And you, Miss—it'll be a kindness, to prove you've no hard feelings.'

'Rolly,' said Gwendoline Fell, some time later, 'I like your friends very much, and they certainly like you. Perhaps I *was* a little hasty when I first talked to you. I think I've reformed.'

'I don't mind you reforming, providing you don't blame me for it,' said Rollison. 'I can't wait to read your column in the morning.'

'If you care to come to Fleet Street, you could see some early editions now,' said Gwendoline.

'Nothing I'd like more,' said Rollison. 'But I've an appointment I mustn't miss. Show an unnatural restraint, Gwendoline—and don't follow me.'

As far as he could judge he was not followed by her or by anyone else on his way to break into Sir Douglas Slatter's house. He called Jolly from a call box and made sure Angela hadn't telephoned; so she had Guy Slatter out somewhere in the West End.

And the big house should be empty, although the police were nearby.

CHAPTER 18

BURGLARY

Rollison drove past both houses. There were two police cars, and policemen were to be seen patrolling the grounds. The front porch of Number 29 was brightly lit and there was a light on in an upstairs room. Rollison parked not far from the spot where he had left his car that afternoon, and walked by a roundabout route across Bloomdale Square towards the back of the house. There were bright lights at Smith Hall, in spite of the fact that it was midnight, but only one light glowed at the back of Slatter's house, and he judged it to be on a landing.

The police were not watching Slatter's; their fears were for the residents of Smith Hall.

Rollison went to the back door of Number 29, and tried the handle; the door yielded, so Angela had done her job.

An inside door was open and a dim light showed. He slipped inside, closed the outer door and entered a large kitchen which led to the passage alongside the stairs. Landing and hall lights were fully on. He opened the doors of the main downstairs rooms, satisfied himself that they were empty, then went upstairs. All landing lights were on, but the house was absolutely silent. He went into the first bedroom he came to. Obviously occupied, a man's clothes were everywhere, on the bed and on the floor; the door of a bathroom, leading off, was open and water dripped from a shower.

Rollison opened cupboards and drawers until he came to

one which was locked. He forced this, without difficulty. His eye lighted on a bundle of letters addressed to Guy Slatter.

Love letters?

He opened two, and each was on the same theme. Both of them were from dead Winifred de Vaux, stating simply that Guy was the father of her child. They went further, and stated with some bitterness that this had happened before to other, many other, unfortunate girls, all of whose illegitimate children Guy had fathered.

Very thoughtful, Rollison went out, leaving the door ajar. He entered a room opposite.

This was obviously Sir Douglas Slatter's room. There was a huge Victorian wardrobe, of some dark, highly polished wood, a dressing table and chest of drawers of the same suite. The wardrobe was where the stockings and gloves had been hidden. Rollison saw a photograph on the dressing-chest, of young Guy taken a few years ago. The likeness between the two men had been quite remarkable, even then. By it was a smaller picture—of Naomi Smith.

Rollison left the door ajar, and began to search.

He found the drawer where the stockings had been kept; Angela had left one behind. In another, immediately above it, were ordinary clothes and underwear. Beneath a hanging section were several pairs of shoes, and Rollison took each pair out and examined it.

On one, were mud stains and splashes; the kind of marks there would quite likely be on the shoes of a man who had run over muddy ground—as Naomi's attacker had run. Rollison put these back, and then looked through the clothes. There was a pair of flannels with mud splashes at the turn-ups, some nearly as high as the knees.

He was putting these back when he heard a sudden furious blaring of horns, not just one or two, but half-a-dozen on different notes. He heard voices, too; shouting and whistling. He went to the window, keeping close to the side, and looked down into the street. A convoy of cars, eight or nine of them, was pulled up in the road, blocking all the traffic in each direction, and youths poured out of them, heading for Smith Hall.

For an awful moment he was afraid the large scale attack he had half-feared had come before Ebbutt's men were here to help. Four policemen appeared in a solid line, blocking the gateway, but three youths rushed into Slatter's drive, and vaulted the wall. They did not go to the front door, but hurled stones at the side door and the windows of Smith Hall, while the honking and bellowing and whistling grew worse.

Rollison ran out of the room, down the stairs to the back door—and saw the youths already on the run; two scared girls were standing at one window, which had a big hole in the middle. Cars snorted and moved off, tyres screeching. From the corner he could see two policemen grappling with some of the youths, who broke away and rushed towards the last car, which was already moving. A man leaned out to drag the youths in, as the cars swung round the corner, engines roaring.

Slowly, silence settled.

Very clearly, a girl's voice sounded:

'I can't stand it, I just can't stand any more!'

It was Judy Lyons.

Someone began to soothe her, someone else called out:

'Nor can I.'

The sound of Naomi's voice followed, calm and clear despite the ugly incident.

'Is anyone hurt? I want to know at once—is anyone hurt?'

No-one had been hurt, it seemed, but Judy was still sobbing, her wails low, persistent and hopeless. Rollison withdrew cautiously. The noise of the invasion had died away, even the distant sound of racing engines had gone. Policemen were talking, and police cars had appeared. One man began to report what had happened as the newcomers drew near and inspected the damage to the windows.

Rollison went back into Slatter's house, and hurried up the stairs. As he reached the main bedroom, it occurred to him that he was using the house almost as if it were his own. He crossed to the photographs and studied them, then tried all the drawers in the room. None was locked. He went across to the study, and saw flashlights down below, heard voices through the window. But hardboard had been placed across the broken pane, there was no danger of him being seen if he were careful. He took a pencil-slim torch from his pocket, twisted the top so that it spread a glow of diffused light, then sat in Slatter's chair and tried the drawers.

The top one was open and the keys were in it. Angela certainly made burglary easy. He paused for a moment, feeling a natural reluctance to intrude on another man's privacy; and then he thought of the girls next door, and of all that had happened, and he opened drawer after drawer without compunction, looking through account books and papers. The more he read, the more he realised Slatter's great wealth, and he spent five minutes poring over one book, obviously kept by Slatter himself, for many years. This was a record of houses and land bought and sold over a long period.

Oct. 10th, 192.. Bought 21 Padfield Road, Fulham,
SW6   £399
Total outgoings over 40 years   £1,070
Total income from rents over 40 years   £4,180
Sold, Oct. 1st, 196.. at a price of   £5,550

On the opposite page were details of tenants and repairs, and general details about the house, offers of purchase and the amounts involved.

This book had a hundred and twenty entries, of houses which Slatter had bought and sold in nearly every part of London. There was a similar book which covered properties in the S.W.1., W.1. and the W.C.1. and W.C.2. areas—at least as many properties, some of them costing a hundred thousand pounds and all sold for at least ten times the purchase price after yielding a substantial income for twenty or more years.

It was easy to think of old Slatter sitting in this very chair and making the entries carefully, with an old-fashioned J-type nib.

Then Rollison came upon a small book, which covered the properties in Bloomdale Street and other streets nearby. Slatter had once owned a whole block of forty-four houses, but had sold them over the years until now he owned only two—this one and the house next door. On the entry for this house was a cryptic:

Offered £45,000 by Bensoni and Tilford . . . refused.

And on the pages covering the house next door, Smith Hall was a similar entry:

Offered £32,500 by Bensoni and Tilford . . . refused.

Both entries had been made only two weeks ago.

Rollison was sitting back, studying these entries and comparing them, recalling all he could of the firm of Bensoni and Tilford, one of the biggest housing and construction companies in Britain, when he heard a giggle. There was no mistaking it—a girl was approaching *up the stairs,* giggling. Almost at once a man said in a harsh whisper:

'Be quiet! There's someone here!'

That was Guy Slatter, and he could not be more than ten yards from the open door of the room. But for Angela's warning giggle, Rollison might have been caught red-handed at the desk.

He did not even push the drawer in, but stood up swiftly and tiptoed towards the door. There was another giggle, much more subdued, from Angela. By then he was standing at the wall alongside the door. He heard a footfall, saw a shadow—and it was remarkably like the shadow which he had seen outside the house next door on the previous night.

Very cautiously, Guy Slatter appeared.

He looked across at the desk, and there was enough light for him to see that the drawers were open and books cluttered the desk. The sight made Guy stride into the room, and as he passed, Rollison struck a chopping blow on the back of his neck—the kind of blow that could kill. Guy staggered forward a few paces, then crumpled up.

Angela appeared almost instantly in the doorway, staring as if dumbstruck at the untidy heap on the floor.

Rollison moved to Guy, bent down, and felt his pulse. It was beating, but he was out cold, and was likely to be for several minutes. Rollison went to the desk and put the book covering this property back into the drawer, placing it beneath the one which was already there, as if the burglar had not had time to inspect that before being disturbed. Angela hadn't moved when Rollison reached her. He put an arm around her waist and hustled her into the passage.

'What brought you back?' he demanded.

'Guy decided he liked me much better at home. Rolly, I tried to keep him away, but——'

'Did he give any special reason?'

'No. No, I don't think so——'

'Angela, my poppet, I think you'd better come with me,' said Rollison. 'You can tell me everything on the way.'

Angela hesitated, and then said: 'I rather like him, Rolly, but I think perhaps you're right. Did you get what you came for?' They were already hurrying down the stairs.

'I think so,' Rollison answered.

'Don't I qualify for the C.I.D.?' Angela demanded.

'You certainly collected the evidence,' Rollison said. They went out the back way and walked in the opposite direction to Smith Hall. No-one appeared to notice them leaving the grounds by the narrow tradesmen's entrance. 'What did happen?'

'Guy had a telephone call at the nightclub,' answered Angela.

'So he left a number where he could be found after you'd persuaded him to take you out,' said Rollison. 'So his mind wasn't entirely on you and romance. Did he answer the call at the table?'

'No, he went out to the foyer,' answered Angela. They reached the Austin A35, and she paused, her voice changing as she asked plaintively: 'If I get into that it won't blow up, will it?'

'I'll lift the bonnet first,' said Rollison and he did so at once, so that the clear light from a street lamp shone on to the engine. 'Nothing there that shouldn't be,' he assured her, opening the door for Angela, then taking the wheel. 'And was he on edge to go as soon as he had the call?'

'No, but he kept looking at his watch,' said Angela.

'What time did the call come through?' asked Rollison.

'About twelve o'clock.'

'That was about the time when Smith Hall had visitors,' remarked Rollison. 'Did he seem pleased or sorry?'

'Oh, pleased,' answered Angela. 'I had the idea that he wanted to be away from the house for a couple of hours, I didn't have to persuade him very hard. And although he kept telling me how beautiful it would be to spend the night alone with me, I can't say he behaved like a gallant lover.'

'When did he say he suspected someone was at the house?' They were moving along Holborn, then, heading for Oxford Street.

'As soon as we came in. He brought me the back way, and when he found the door open he became suspicious. After all, that *was* natural. Rolly, did you really find out anything that matters? Did you find any other evidence that it was Sir Douglas who tried to attack Naomi Smith?'

'Good lord, no!' exclaimed Rollison.

She gaped up at him.

'But—but——'

'His clothes were mud-stained and the things were in his wardrobe, but he hadn't worn them,' Rollison said. 'He couldn't possibly have moved at speed, and would probably have broken his arm if he'd jarred it against mine like the attacker did. No, it wasn't Sir Douglas. He could possibly have another nephew who could get into his clothes, and put them back in his wardrobe, but I don't think it very likely.'

'You mean—*Guy* was going to kill Naomi?'

'There's certainly a possibility that he was,' answered Rollison. 'But I don't believe he's the moving spirit behind all this, although he *may* have murdered the four victims. We need to find the influence and the pressures behind Guy Slatter,' added Rollison, as he pulled up outside his house in Gresham Terrace. 'I wonder,' he went on almost as if speaking to himself, 'whether there is a Mr. Bensoni or a Mr. Tilford in the firm.'

144

'What on earth made you ask *that?*' cried Angela. 'The man who telephoned him was named Bensoni. I heard the head waiter say so. "Mr. Bensoni is on the line," he said. I haven't any doubt at all.'

CHAPTER 19

BUSY MORNING

Jolly was still up, the trophies on the wall glowed under special lighting; Angela, though wide-eyed, gave a gargantuan yawn.

'Ring Grice at the Yard,' Rollison said to Jolly. 'If he's not there, call him at home. Angela, pet, if you want to be up in time to greet the morning you'd better go to bed.'

He stopped her in the middle of another yawn.

'Not until I know what you're up to,' Angela said. 'Why is Bensoni——'

He patted her head with insufferable condescension as he passed on the way to the bathroom. When he came back, Angela was sitting, dwarfed, in his huge chair, and Jolly, looking rather like a rehabilitated mummy, was at the telephone.

'Mr. Grice's home number is ringing, sir.'

'Thanks.' Rollison took the telephone as Grice growled a discouraging 'Hallo'.

'I'm sorry about this, Bill,' Rollison said in his warmest tone. 'But I did promise to keep you informed.'

'Then inform me,' Grice said coldly.

'The man who attacked Naomi Smith was Guy Slatter, and——'

'*Mister* Rollison,' interrupted Grice, 'you didn't wake me up in the middle of the night to tell me the obvious, did you? We have been pretty sure it was Guy Slatter all the time, but we can't yet establish that he killed anyone. From his reputation, we're fairly certain that he's not capable of running this by himself, certainly not of arranging for a gang of young ruffians to attack the hostel as they did tonight.'

'I heard a rumour about that,' murmured Rollison. 'And I didn't ring you simply to give you the name of the murderer. Someone slipped up badly tonight, and Guy had a call from a certain Mr. Bensoni.' There was a moment of silence, as if Grice were trying to see the significance of the name; and then his voice rose almost to shrillness. 'Bensoni and Tilford!'

'Builders, construction engineers and estate developers,' said Rollison earnestly. 'They, at least, are used to organising demolition gangs and so forth, and there are already flats in construction on a nearby site.'

'Are you absolutely certain about this?' demanded Grice.

'I am certain that Guy was called to a telephone by a man said to be Mr. Bensoni, while at a nightclub—what nightclub, Angela?'

'The Hip-Strip,' called Angela promptly.

'The Hip-Strip, in Soho,' said Rollison. 'I also know that he then began to agitate to get back to the house. What happened when he got there, according to my niece Angela, is that he nearly caught a burglar and the burglar got away.'

'I wonder who that burglar was,' said Grice, drily. 'Where are you?'

'At home—and I do not want to go to the Hip-Strip Club,' declared Rollison. 'I want to go to bed, because I think it's going to be a very busy morning. That house is being closely watched, isn't it?'

'Not closely enough,' admitted Grice. 'But it soon will be. Goodnight.'

Rollison put down the receiver as a miniature striking clock on the mantelpiece struck two. Angela rose slowly from the chair and peered up into Rollison's face, like a trusting child.

'So I'm not such a bad detective,' she remarked.

'You have eyes like a hawk and ears like a bat's,' answered Rollison. 'Now you have to prove you can manage with four hours' sleep.'

'Oh, that's plenty for young people,' declared Angela, and skipped away to dodge his descending hand.

147

It was full daylight when he woke, to find Jolly by his side proffering tea and the *Daily Globe* on a tray; Jolly must have been out to get a copy as early as this. Rollison struggled up —as the miniature clock struck six. He felt a little heavy in the head and behind the eyes, but all that had happened and all that might happen today flooded through his mind by the time he was sitting up and opening the newspaper, while Jolly poured his tea.

'Shall I call Miss Angela, sir? She is very soundly asleep.'

'Give her another twenty minutes,' said Rollison. 'I want to be off by seven.'

'To the hostel, sir?'

'To check with Grice, check with Ebbutt, and then get to Bloomdale Street,' answered Rollison. 'I—my! They've certainly made it the story of the day!'

There, on the tabloid front page, was a picture of Sir Douglas Slatter, of the shattered window and of the house next door. The headlines screamed:

Attack on Millionaire
Vengeful Unwed Mother Heaves Brick

'And if that isn't actionable I won't have breakfast,' said Rollison. He looked down the page to a picture of Anne Miller holding a baby, and the caption beneath this read:

Charged with Malicious Wounding

The story of the hostel and the feud between the residents and Slatter was told brilliantly, in detail. There was one paragraph set in bold type, which read:

Mrs. Naomi Smith, Superintendent of the hostel, was viciously attacked by an unknown man outside the hostel. One of the residents is known to have been murdered. Two of the trustees have been murdered, also.

In the *Stop Press*, in red, was another paragraph.

Gang of youths attacked Smith Hall, residence for unmarried mothers in Bloomdale Street. Police drove attackers off. See story p. 1.

Slowly, almost reluctantly, Rollison turned to page three, where Gwendoline's column always appeared. There was her photograph, and further down the page was a photograph of Naomi Smith outside Smith Hall.

The column was headed:

Strong Man Relents

The story read:

Sir Douglas Slatter, multi-millionaire, philanthropist and property owner, could have brought despair to twenty-three mothers or mothers-to-be.

And Sir Douglas, strictly religious—some might say a religious bigot—has always said that if a young woman is unmarried when she has a child, she has cast herself out of society.

Twenty-five of these 'outcasts' lived next door to him in a mansion in Bloomdale Street, close to the University of London and the British Museum. Sir Douglas owns the property. He ordered, sternly, 'out!'

Now, one of the unweds has been murdered, and another is missing.

And now Sir Douglas, the strictly religious multi-millionaire, has relented. The remaining twenty-three will not be cast out. This multi-millionaire's heart of stone melted. I salute him.

I wish I could also salute the police. Three people have been brutally murdered. All of them are closely connected with the Bloomdale Street mansion.

Why have no arrests been made?

What is the mystery behind this home where not only mothers and mothers-to-be should live in happiness—but where babies, under 12 months old, now live under threat of hideous death?

Rollison finished his tea as Jolly looked in, and said:
'Your bath is ready, sir.'

'Yes. Did you read Gwendoline Fell's column?'

'Very pungent indeed, sir,' Jolly said, as if with approval.

'I can't think of a better word,' said Rollison. He lifted the telephone next to his bed and dialled Bill Ebbutt's number at the Blue Dog. Almost immediately a woman answered in a bright Cockney voice.

'Mrs. Ebbutt speaking.'

'Hallo, Liz,' said Rollison. 'I'm glad I didn't get you up.'

'Goodness me, no—I've been up since five o'clock, that's my usual time. And for once Bill got up early, too, he left just after six. Said it was something to do with you, Mister Ar, and that hostel that's all over the front page. Poor little mites. And the mothers, too, as if they haven't got enough to worry about. Always coming up against this problem in the Army, but you know that. Well, I suppose I mustn't keep you, but there's one thing I would like to ask you, Mr. Ar. If ever that young woman Gwendoline comes over here again, I want to meet her. Wouldn't it be lovely if she would do a story about the Army?'

'Liz,' said Rollison warmly, 'it would be wonderful. I'll talk to her about it. Goodbye.' He rang off before she could get another word in, and then saw his door open a fraction, and Angela's head appear. She looked half-asleep and so very young.

'It's me,' she said. 'Do I have time for breakfast?'

'Provided you don't wolf mine,' said Rollison. 'I——' He broke off, as his telephone bell rang, and Angela came further into the room. She wore a pale pink quilted dressing gown which was too large for her. 'Rollison,' Rollison said into the telephone.

'Rolly,' said Grice, in a very hard voice, 'were you at Slatter's house last night?'

Something in his manner told Rollison that the question had grave significance. He could lie, and perhaps never be found out, but if the police had to investigate then Angela would become involved in the lie, and he would break faith with Grice—who had probably assumed that he had been in

150

Bloomdale Street. It seemed a long time before he answered, and while Angela's eyes grew clearer, the sleepy mist faded.

Then he said: 'Yes, Bill.'

'Did you attack Guy Slatter?'

'I hit him on the back of the neck—yes.'

'Did you hit him with a sledge hammer and break his skull?' asked Grice.

Rollison caught his breath.

'Good God, no! Is he—dead?'

'Yes. I had the house watched to make sure no-one went in or out, and no-one did, from ten minutes after your telephone call. When the daily staff went in at half-past six, they found him lying near his uncle's desk, dead—killed like the others. I think you'd better come over at once, and make a statement.'

'I'll be there inside an hour,' Rollison promised.

He looked steadily at Angela as he replaced the receiver. She had moved very slowly towards him, and was now within arm's reach of the bed.

'Guy?' she asked.

'I'm afraid so.'

'Did—did *you* kill him?'

'Did you see a hammer in my hand?' asked Rollison.

'Oh, my God! *That* way?'

'That way. Angela, listen to me.' He took her hands. 'I broke into Slatter's house last night. You did not leave the door open and you did not tell me where to find the keys. You can tell the police I asked you to persuade Guy to take you out. You can even tell them you guessed why, but you took no active part in helping me. Do you understand? If the police know that, they can make a lot of unpleasantness for you without it helping me at all. *Do* you understand?'

Very slowly, she answered: 'Yes.' She tried to free her hand but could not and that told him how tightly he was gripping. He relaxed a little, then said in a more casual voice: 'If you still want to come, we've half-an-hour.'

'Just try to keep me away!' exclaimed Angela, and she pivoted round and ran out of the room.

Rollison almost laughed, but there was nothing even remotely funny about the situation, and there were probably dangers which he hadn't yet seen. Had he been watched at Slatter's house? Had someone seen him go in and seen him leave with Angela, then gone in and slugged Guy, leaving him dead?

It seemed likely.

Mechanically turning bathroom taps on and off, vigorously towelling, Rollison knew that Guy would not have stayed unconscious from the chopping blow for more than ten or fifteen minutes at the outside. Someone, then, must have gone in almost immediately after they had left. He was sure no-one had followed them, but not sure they hadn't been watched.

Steam clouded the mirrors and Rollison pushed open the window. As he did so, he caught sight of a movement in the courtyard below.

Two men were stepping on to the bottom platform of the iron fire escape. They were not tradesmen; they were tough-looking; and they wore workmen's clothes. Leaving the open window, Rollison moved swiftly into the living-room. Here he could see the road.

A battered-looking car had just pulled up. Two men got out, waited for a milk-float to pass, then crossed towards Rollison's house and disappeared. Almost at the same time, a motor-cyclist pulled up, fifty yards along; he did not get off his machine but straddled it, as if he were on the lookout.

Jolly appeared, at the dining-alcove.

'Would you—is there anything the matter, sir?'

'Yes,' said Rollison. 'Call Grice at once, tell him I think we're going to be attacked.'

'Attacked——' Jolly began, and then darted towards the telephone. Rollison went as swiftly to the front door. It had been unbolted, but he shot the bolts and put the chain up; and the door was reinforced and almost impossible to break down.

He spun round.

'The telephone is dead, sir,' Jolly stated in an even voice.

Rollison stared—and then hurried towards the back door. He thought he heard footsteps just outside as he rammed the bolts home, then stretched up and put shutters up at the small windows alongside the door. There had been a time when raids on this flat were commonplace, and everything had been reinforced.

There was a heavy knock at the back door.

'It looks as if someone has tumbled to the fact that Angela and I might know too much for their safety,' Rollison said. 'They're pretty slow—and I had the bodyguards sent to the wrong place. If this crowd really means business—and I've seen four who look as if they do—we're really in trouble. They could have that door down in ten seconds flat with a single charge of dynamite. And they've used dynamite at least once before.'

As he finished there was another knock at the back door, and a long, loud ring at the front.

Angela appeared, fully dressed, fresh and pink-cheeked. 'Who on earth is that?' she asked in a voice not far from scared.

'The knell of doom,' said Rollison, knowing that she would want no punches pulled. He went to his desk and unlocked the master drawer at the top, took out a small, grey pistol which did not look large enough to cause injury. 'I think whoever is behind this knows that you heard the name Bensoni, and might have passed word on to me. They know I'm supposed always to be a lone wolf, and they'll expect me to try to handle this on my own. So they've come to make sure I can't—*and* to make sure you can't pass word on to the police.'

A thunderous knocking drowned the last words, and then clearly from the letter box in the front door, a man called out in a rough, uneducated voice:

'We know you're in there, Rollison. Open the door or we'll blow it down.'

CHAPTER 20

BIG BLAST

'I see what you mean,' said Angela in a small voice.

'Rollison!' roared the man outside.

'Coming!' called the Toff, as if he hadn't a worry in the world. He whispered to Angela: 'This is tear-gas. Go and help Jolly.' Jolly, with some cigarettes in his hand, also taken from the drawer, was heading for the kitchen.

Angela cast a longing look at Rollison, then went after Jolly.

Rollison reached the front door. The men outside were silent now, quite unaware that they could be seen. Above the front door was a kind of periscope mirror, and glancing up Rollison saw the two who had come from the car standing outside—and two others halfway down the stairs. One of them was laying a trail of gunpowder.

The man nearest to the door bent down, and poked a finger at the letter box.

'Rollison!' he roared. 'This is your last chance. Open the door!'

'Just about to,' answered Rollison. He poked the muzzle of the gas pistol through the letter box, squeezed the trigger, and heard the hiss and a cry of alarm, then a thud as the man at the box fell. He fired two more capsules of the tear gas, felt a blow-back of it bite at his nose and eyes—and he heard another man cry out:

'Gawd!'

Yet another gave a choking scream.

154

Rollison unlocked and unchained the door in three swift movements. On the landing two men were reeling, and another was sprawling halfway down the stairs. The one with the dynamite was backing away, a hazy figure through the gas. Rollison closed his eyes and mouth, nipped his nostrils, and rushed downwards. When he opened his eyes again the man hurled the dynamite at him, then turned and rushed down the second flight of stairs. Rollison simply levelled the gun and the pellet hit the stairs and burst in front of the escaping man.

On the next landing was yet another assailant.

And in his hand was a sledge hammer.

He raised it, to throw, alarm showing in his eyes. Rollison ducked. The hammer flew over his head and crashed against the wall. Instead of using the pistol, which contained two more pellets, Rollison hurled himself at the man, both fists clenched; he had never struck a chin with greater force, and the man simply toppled backwards and slid, head-first, down the next flight of stairs.

At this point the door of one of the flats opened, and an elderly tenant demanded in a deep and authoritative voice:

'What the devil is going on here?'

'Call the police,' Rollison said, over his shoulder. 'Call——'

Then the front door burst open and half-a-dozen men rushed in, enough to have struck terror even into the Toff but for the sight of Bill Ebbutt, leading the way. In Bill's hand was an old-fashioned black leather cosh, once regarded as a deadly weapon but a toy compared with knuckle-dusters, bicycle chains, iron bars and flick knives. The elderly neighbour withdrew hastily and slammed his door. One of the fallen men crawled to his feet, then backed against the wall, his hands raised.

'Any of your boys at the back?' asked Rollison.

Ebbutt looked up, mouth wide open.

'Gorblimey; Mr. Ar, I thought you was a goner. You okay?' The broadest of grins nearly spit his face in two. 'I don't need any telling. I should have known. Strewth, Mr. Ar——'

'Are any of your chaps at the back?' interrupted Rollison with greater urgency.

'Six,' answered Ebbutt. 'I should've known you——'

He broke off and lunged past Rollison, who turned round in alarm, but it was only one of the men whom he had gassed, coming down the stairs a step at a time, tears streaming from his eyes. Behind him came Angela, a handkerchief over her nose and mouth, her eyes tear-filled. She stopped halfway down the stairs at the sight of Ebbutt, who touched his forehead and said smartly:

'Good morning, Miss. I—*strewth*. It's Miss Angela, I didn't recognise you for a moment.' He pushed forward and gripped Angela's hand—and as he pumped her arm up and down, Jolly appeared, and asked in a voice hoarsened by the tear gas:

'Is everything satisfactory here, sir?'

'Yes, Jolly,' Rollison said. 'What about the back?'

'The situation is quite under control,' Jolly assured him. 'We need the telephone repaired of course, but apart from that all is well. *Good* morning, Mr. Ebbutt.'

'Hallo, Jolly me old cock,' wheezed Ebbutt, squeezing Jolly's hand in turn. 'I might have guessed. Mr. Ar had torn a strip off them before we got here. Came the minute we learned——' He broke off, as the others stared at Rollison and Rollison looked as if he was appalled. 'What's up, Mr. Ar? What's the matter?'

'You were to have been at Smith Hall,' Rollison said in a hoarse voice. 'Those girls——'

'Oh, don't you worry about those little angels,' said Ebbutt, bluffly. 'Old Bill Grice isn't so bad when you get used to him. There was a demolition charge under the house, all set to go off at seven *ack emma*, but Grice had the place combed. Found the charge underneath the kitchen, the whole place would have been wrecked, Gawd knows what we could have done to help the little loves. But it's okay. Caught a couple of chaps, too. They say it was done by Guy Slatter or whatever his name is. Was, I mean. But one of them had a sledge hammer in his sack, and the hammer was the one used to crown Guy. Grice will sew it all up now, Mr. Ar, don't you worry.'

'What brought you here?' asked Rollison.

'Well as a matter of fact, Mr. Ar, we caught one of the slickers when he was sneaking away.' Ebbutt raised and

156

clenched his fist, and it looked like a small ham. 'I persuaded him to talk a bit, and he said they was going to blow *your* place up. Said something about you finding out who was behind it and they were going to shut your trap. Mr. Grice and the cops were busy, so we got a move on here. But I should've known,' he went on with that enormous grin. 'You didn't need us.'

'I never needed you so much,' said Rollison. He gripped Bill Ebbutt's shoulder for what seemed a long time, and then turned to Angela. 'Why don't you stay and help Jolly clear up?' he suggested. 'I've got to see Grice but I don't think you'll find it very interesting.'

'Rolly,' said Angela, in a small voice, 'I don't want to be a detective any more. But you—you were *wonderful*. You——' She stood on tiptoe and kissed him. 'You really were!'

'What I don't understand,' said Grice, half-an-hour later, 'is why you were so sure there was to be an attack on Smith Hall.'

'I didn't see how it could be avoided,' Rollison replied. He was standing in the cellar of the house, where the charge of dynamite had been discovered. 'Savage murders galore, and millions obviously at stake. They had done their absolute damnedest to get everyone out of the house, and they weren't going to stop at anything. When they had reason to believe that Slatter would relent, they had to make a final grand slam, and we knew life didn't mean anything to them—other people's, that is. I didn't know what they would do but I was sure it would be something disastrous and final.'

Grice, looking saturnine in the dimly-lit cellar, nodded for him to continue.

'It was pretty clear that they would need a scapegoat, a man who would take the blame,' Rollison went on. 'Guy Slatter was the obvious one. He had been involved: he may or may not have committed the murders, but they could certainly be traced to him.'

'And what motive could he have?' asked Grice. 'It would have to be a big one, to be convincing.'

'Oh, that was simple enough,' said Rollison. 'He was the
157

heir to Sir Douglas Slatter, who was holding out on the sale of this house and the one next door. Bensoni and Tilford had bought every other piece of property on this block. Once they had the lot, they could sell it for millions—but Sir Douglas had enough millions and didn't want any more.'

'Very interesting,' said Grice. 'But if Guy were going to inherit his uncle's millions anyway, why should he help Bensoni and Tilford—or whoever was involved?'

'Sir Douglas had strong views about young people who had children without first getting married,' answered Rollison. 'Guy's view was far less rigid—so much so that the evidence of it could have caused his uncle to leave his money elsewhere. One of Guy's girls was Winifred de Vaux, and I don't doubt she'd told Webberson. I can only guess that Webberson tried to make Guy influence his uncle. I imagine that was how Webberson and gentle Dr. Brown became involved, and thus, a danger to Guy, who feared disinheritance if the truth came out. Remember how Naomi Smith was so sure their troubles were over—before the murders. Keith may well have told her he could and would bring pressure to bear on Sir Douglas Slatter.'

'Yes,' agreed Grice, hesitantly. 'Yes, I suppose it all fits in. You can fill in gaps with your imagination which I can't fill in without evidence. But there is one piece of evidence which you'll find very interesting.'

'What is it?' asked Rollison.

'The firm of Bensoni and Tilford is on the rocks,' said Grice. 'Labour troubles and the loss of some big contracts led to it. They needed the Bloomdale site desperately. They've borrowed to the hilt on the other properties, and Sir Douglas Slatter's refusal to sell was likely to ruin them. I can tell you another thing,' Grice went on, after a pause. 'Guy's telephone call last night wasn't from Bensoni. It was from the foreman of the gang which raided your place. Guy, knowing of the impending raid, told him to ring him at the club if it were successful. The man gave Bensoni's name rather than risk his own. No doubt he invented some inducement to get Guy back to the house, where he intended to murder him. It is possible that it was he who committed one or more of the earlier murders, and Guy knew of it.'

'It could be,' conceded Rollison. 'The fatal flaw in criminality, that each must trust the other. Do you—er—do you want me for anything else?'

'No,' said Grice. 'Not for a while. Naomi Smith would like to see you.'

'I'd like a word with her, too,' said Rollison. 'What about Anne Miller?'

'She'll be remanded for a week,' Grice said, 'and then be bound over as a first offender. She's lucky, in a way.'

'Yes,' said Rollison. 'I suppose she is.'

He went up to the ground floor, a little surprised to see no-one about, tapped at the door of Naomi Smith's room, went in on her call—and stood aghast on the threshold. For every single one of the girls was there, and every single one rose spontaneously, and began to cheer. Then they rushed forward to surround him, each in turn giving him a demonstrative hug. When at last Naomi had called them off, and they were gone, he was quite breathless.

'I've never known them so happy,' Naomi said. 'Never known them so eager to work, either. And they're *quite* sure that you'll get them out of their troubles one way or another. So am I,' she added. 'So am I.'

'Naomi,' said Rollison, firmly, 'you have always known more than you've admitted.'

'Nothing that I believed could affect the case,' Naomi said. 'But yes—I did, Richard.' She had never used his Christian name before. 'I guessed for instance that Guy Slatter was the father of Anne Miller's child. She never disclosed that, though she hated him and hated Sir Douglas. I guessed, too, that she had intercepted the letter, and was at my wits end to know how to shield her. *Can* you help her?'

'Yes,' said Rollison, and told her what Grice had said.

'I'm so very glad,' said Naomi. 'So deeply grateful, too. When it began, of course, Keith and George Brown knew Guy was a profligate, and could prove it. They believed that to avoid disclosure, Guy could use his influence with his uncle to renew the lease. Afterwards——'

159

'You should have told the police,' said Rollison sternly.

'Oh, I did,' said Naomi unhappily. 'And it was in the letter I wrote to you that Anne intercepted.'

'I see,' Rollison said heavily, and stood up. As he looked down at her, his gaze was kindly and understanding. 'How is Douglas this morning. Do you know?'

'I'm told he's recovered from the shock, and I'm going to see him soon,' Naomi said. 'I can only hope that this new shock won't cause a serious relapse.'

Naomi telephoned Rollison, later, to say that Sir Douglas had taken the blow well.

And Grice telephoned, also, to say that Iris Jay had been found, safe but in hiding, and that Bensoni had confessed complicity but blamed the murders on to Guy and the foreman ganger: sorting the details out was only a matter of time.

And in time, Bensoni was tried and found guilty and sentenced to life imprisonment.

So was the foreman, whom Rollison saw for the first time when he went to give evidence at the trial.

And a little later, Rollison went to a very different ceremony, with Angela and Gwendoline Fell, with twenty-five girls including Anne Miller, and with Naomi Smith—who, on that day, married Sir Douglas Slatter. She had solved the problem of the noise and his studies very simply indeed.

Sir Douglas now had his study on the other side of the house, where no children cried.